# GRIMMS' FAIRY TALES

# GRIMMS'
# FAIRY TALES

### Book 1

*Illustrated by*
CHARLES FOLKARD

J. M. Dent & Sons Limited   London

*JAKOB GRIMM was born in 1785 and his brother Wilhelm a year later. Jakob died in 1863 and Wilhelm in 1857.*

*They were born at Hanau in Germany and educated at Marburg University. Both were subsequently on the staff of Göttingen University and later moved to Berlin.*

*As quite young men the brothers began a life's work of research into the folklore of their country, listening to and writing down legends and stories as they heard them in the cottages of the peasants, in village inns and country places. They discovered material in medieval MSS. preserved in libraries and museums, and keeping strictly to the originals made their world-famous collections of fairy and folk tales.*

*Jakob was the stronger of the brothers, for Wilhelm was often compelled to lead an invalid's life. They were devoted friends, and were never separated, for when Wilhelm married, Jakob came to live with him and his wife. Both were learned scholars.*

*First published in Dent Dolphins 1977*

*Made in Great Britain at*
*The Aldine Press, Letchworth, Hertfordshire*
*for J. M. Dent & Sons Limited*
*Aldine House, Albemarle Street, London*

ISBN 0 460 02730 1

# CONTENTS

# The Dancing Shoes

A KING once had twelve most beautiful daughters. They slept in twelve beds, all in a row, in one room: and when they went to bed the king always went up and shut and locked the door. But for all this care that was taken of them, their shoes were every morning found to be quite worn through, as if they had been danced in all night; and yet nobody could find out how it happened, or where they could have been.

Then the king made it known to all the land, that if anybody could find out where it was that the princesses danced in the night that man should have the one he liked best of the whole twelve for wife, and should be king after his death; but that whoever tried, and could not, after three days and nights, discover the truth, should be put to death.

A king's son soon came. He was well lodged and fed, and in the evening was taken to the chamber next to the one where the princesses lay in their twelve beds. There he was to sit and watch where they went to dance; and in order that nothing might pass without his hearing it, the door of their chamber was left open. But the prince soon fell asleep; and when he awoke in the morning he found that the princesses had all been dancing, for the soles of their shoes were full of holes. The same thing happened the second and third nights: so the king had his head cut off without mercy.

After him came many others; but they all had the same luck, and lost their lives in the same way.

Now it chanced that a poor soldier, who had been wounded in battle and could fight no longer, passed through this country; and as he was travelling through a wood he met a little old woman, who asked him where he was going. 'I hardly know where I am going, or what I had better do,' said the soldier, and added for a joke: 'But I think I should like very much to find out where it is that these princesses dance, and then I might have a wife, and in time I might be a king.' 'Well, well,' said the old woman, nodding her head. 'That is no very hard task: only take care not to drink the wine that one of the princesses will bring to you in the evening; and as soon as she leaves you you must seem to fall fast asleep.'

Then she gave him a cloak, and said: 'As soon as you put that on you will become invisible; and you will then be able to follow the princesses wherever they go, without their being aware of it.' When the soldier heard this he thought he would try his luck in earnest: so he took courage, went to the king, and said he was willing to undertake the task.

He was as well lodged as the others had been, and the king ordered fine royal robes to be given him; and when the evening came he was led to the outer chamber. Just as he was going to lie down the eldest of the princesses brought him a cup of wine; but the soldier had tied a sponge under his chin, and let it soak into that, taking care not to drink a drop. Then he laid himself down on his bed, and in a little while began to snore very loud, as if he was fast asleep. When the twelve princesses heard this they all laughed heartily; and the eldest said: 'This fellow too might have done a wiser thing than lose his life in this way!' Then they rose up and opened their cupboards and chests and boxes, and took out all their fine clothes and dressed themselves before the mirror; put on the twelve pairs of new shoes that the king had just bought them, and skipped about as if they were eager to begin dancing. But the youngest said: 'I don't know how it is, but though you are so happy I feel very uneasy; I am sure some mischance will befall us.' 'You simpleton!' said the eldest, 'you are always afraid; have you forgotten how many kings' sons have already watched us in vain? As for this soldier, he had one eye shut already, when he came into the room; and even if I had not given him his sleeping draught he would have slept soundly enough.'

When they were ready they went and looked at the soldier; but he snored on, and did not stir a hand or foot, so they thought they were quite safe; and the eldest went up to her own bed, and clapped her hands, and the bed sank into the floor, and a trap-door flew open. The soldier saw them going down through the trap-door, one after another, the eldest leading the way; and thinking he had no time to lose he jumped up, and put on the cloak which the old fairy had given him, and followed them.　Half-way down the stairs he trod on the gown of the youngest, and she cried out: 'All is not well; someone took hold of my gown.'　'You silly thing!' said the eldest; 'it was nothing but a nail in the wall.'

Then down they all went, and they found themselves in a most delightful avenue of trees; and the leaves were all of silver, and glittered and sparkled beautifully.　The soldier wished to take away some token of the place; so he broke off a little branch, and there came a loud crack from the tree.　Then the youngest daughter said again: 'I am sure all is not right: did you not hear that noise?　That never happened before.'　But the eldest said: 'It is only the princes, who are shouting for joy at our approach.'

They soon came to another grove of trees, where all the leaves were of gold; and afterwards to a third, where the leaves were all glittering diamonds.　And the soldier broke a twig from each; and every time there came a loud noise that made the youngest sister shiver with fear: but the eldest still said it was the princes who were shouting for joy.　So they went on till they came to a great lake; and at the side of the lake there lay twelve little boats, with a handsome prince in each, waiting for the princesses.

One of the princesses went into each boat, and the soldier stepped into the same boat with the youngest.　As they were rowing over the lake the prince who was in the boat with the youngest princess and the soldier said: 'I do not know how it is; though I am rowing with all my might we get on very slowly, and I am quite tired: the boat seems very heavy to-day, especially at one end.'　'It is only the heat of the weather,' said the princess; 'I feel it very warm too.'

On the other side of the lake stood a fine illuminated castle, from which came merry music of drums and trumpets. There they all landed and went into the castle, and each prince danced with his princess; and the soldier, who was all the time invisible, danced with them too; and when any of the princesses had a cup of wine set by her, he drank it all up, so that when she put the cup to her lips it was empty. At this, too, the youngest sister was sadly frightened; but the eldest always silenced her. They danced on till three o'clock in the morning, and then all their shoes were worn out, so that they were forced to leave off. The princes rowed them back over the lake; but this time the soldier sat himself in the boat by the eldest princess, and her prince too found it very hard work to row that night. On the other shore they all took leave saying they would come again the next night.

When they came to the stairs the soldier ran on before the princesses, and laid himself down; and as they came up slowly, panting for breath and very much tired, they heard him snoring in his bed, and said: 'Now all is quite safe.' Then they undressed themselves, put away their fine clothes, pulled off their shoes, and went to bed, and to sleep.

In the morning the soldier said nothing about what had happened, for he wished to see more of this sport. So he went again the second night, and everything happened just as before, the princesses dancing each time till their shoes were worn to pieces, and then going home tired; but the third night the soldier carried away one of the golden cups, as a token of where he had been.

On the morning of the fourth day he was ordered to appear before the king; so he took with him the three twigs and the golden cup. The twelve princesses stood listening behind the door to hear what he would say, laughing within themselves to think how cleverly they had taken him in, as well as all the rest who had watched them. Then the king asked him: 'Where do my twelve daughters dance at night?' And the soldier said: 'With twelve princes in a castle underground.' So he told the king all that had happened, and showed him the three twigs and the golden cup that he had brought with him. On this the king called for the princesses, and asked them whether what the soldier said was true or not; and when they saw they were found out, and that it was of no use to deny what had happened, they said it was all true.

Then the king asked the soldier which of them he would choose for his wife; and he said: 'I am not very young, so I think I had better take the eldest.' And they were married that very day, and the soldier was declared heir to the kingdom, after the king, his father-in-law, should die.

But as for the princes, they were awarded punishment for as many days as they had danced by night with the princesses.

# The House in the Wood

A POOR woodcutter lived with his wife and three
daughters in a little cottage on the edge of a lonely
forest. One morning, as he was setting out to work, he
said to his wife: 'Let our eldest daughter bring my dinner
out to me in the forest, for I shan't have time to come home
for it. And so that she does not lose her way,' he added, 'I
will take a bag of millet with me, and scatter the grains
behind me as I go.'

7

Now when the sun was high over the forest the girl set out with a bowl of soup. But the sparrows, the larks, the finches, the starlings, and the tits had long since pecked up all the millet, so that the girl could not find a trace of her father. So she followed her nose until the sun went down and night came on. The trees rustled in the darkness, the owls hooted, and she began to be frightened. Far away she saw a light shining behind the trees. 'There must be people there,' she thought. 'Perhaps they will take me in for the night.' So she went towards the light. It was not long before she came to a house, from the window of which the light was shining. She knocked at the door, and a rough voice from inside called out: 'Come in!' She went into the dark porch and knocked on the parlour door. 'Do come in!' called the voice, and when she opened the door there was an old man with hair as grey as ice sitting at the table, with his head on his hands, and his white beard flowing over the table and almost down to the floor.

Three creatures were lying by the stove; a hen, a cock, and a brindled cow. The girl told the old man her plight, and asked him for shelter for the night. He said:

> 'Pretty cock, pretty hen,
> What say you then?
> Pretty brindled cow,
> What say you now?'

'Dux!' they answered: and that must have meant: 'We are willing,' because the old man went on: 'Here 's enough and to spare; go to the kitchen range and cook us some supper.' In the kitchen she found plenty of everything, and she cooked a good meal, but never thought of the animals. She carried the dishes to the table, sat down with the old man, and ate till her hunger was satisfied. When she had finished she said: 'I am so tired now, where is a bed, on which I can lie down and sleep?' The creatures answered:

> 'Since with him you sat drinking
> And eating, never thinking
> Of us and of our hungry plight,
> Now see where you shall spend the night!'

'Just go upstairs,' said the old man, 'and you will find a room with two beds in it. Shake up the beds and cover them with clean linen. Then I shall come up, too, and go to bed.' So she went upstairs and shook up the beds, and put clean sheets on, and lay down in one of them without waiting for the old man. Some time after that he came up, looked at her by the light of a candle, and shook his head. When he saw that she was fast asleep, he opened a trap-door, and dropped her down into the cellar.

Late in the evening the woodcutter came home and reproached his wife for letting him go hungry all day. 'It is not my fault,' she answered, 'the girl went out with your dinner, and must have lost her way. She'll come back in the morning.' The woodcutter got up before it was light, got ready to go to work, and said that their second daughter was to bring his dinner out to him, this time. 'I will take a bag of lentils with me,' he said, 'for they are bigger than grains of millet. The girl will see them, and cannot miss the way.' At midday she carried his dinner out, but the lentils had vanished. As on the day before, the birds of the forest had pecked them all up, and not left one behind. The girl wandered about the forest until it was dark, and she too came to the house where the old man lived, was invited in, and asked for

supper and a bed.   The man with the white beard again
asked the creatures:

> 'Pretty cock, pretty hen,
> What say you then?
> Pretty brindled cow
> What say you now?'

Again they answered 'Dux!' and all happened just as
the day before.   The girl cooked a good supper, ate and
drank with the old man, and took no thought for the
animals.   When she asked where she was to spend the
night they answered:

> 'Since with him you sat drinking
> And eating, never thinking
> Of us and of our hungry plight
> Now see where you shall spend the night!'

When she had gone to sleep the old man came and looked
at her, shaking his head, and tipped her down the cellar.

On the third morning the woodcutter said to his wife:
'To-day you must send our youngest daughter out with
my dinner.   She has always been good and obedient, she
will stay on the right track, and not stray about like those
wild hoydens, her sisters.'   Her mother was loath to
send her, and said: 'Am I now to lose the dearest of my
children, too?'   'Have no fear,' he said, 'the girl will not
lose her way, she is too clever and sensible.   Besides, I
will take peas with me, and scatter them behind me; they
are even bigger than lentils, and they will mark the way
for her.'   But when she set out with her basket on her arm
the wood-pigeons had got their crops full of peas, and she

did not know which way to turn. She grew very anxious, thinking of her poor father going hungry and her mother worrying, if she stayed out late. At last, when it was dark, she saw the little light and came to the house in the wood. She asked politely if she might spend the night there, and the man with the white beard asked his creatures:

> 'Pretty cock, pretty hen,
> What say you then?
> Pretty brindled cow,
> What say you now?'

'Dux!' they said. Then the girl went to the stove, where they were lying, and caressed the cock and the hen, stroking their smooth feathers with her hand, and scratched the brindled cow between her horns. When she had done as the old man told her, and cooked a good supper, and the plates of soup were on the table, she said: 'Am I to eat my fill and give the poor animals nothing? There's plenty for them to eat outside. I'll feed them first.' She went and fetched barley, and scattered it in front of the cock and the hen, and brought an armful of fragrant hay for the cow. 'Eat away, dear creatures,' she said, 'and if you are thirsty you shall have a drink too.' She brought in a pail of fresh water, and the cock and the hen jumped up on to the rim, and dipped their beaks in the water and held their heads in the air, as birds do when they drink, and the brindled cow took a deep draught too. When the beasts were fed and watered, the girl sat down with the old man at the table, and ate what he had left for her. Before long the cock and the hen began to put their heads under their wings, and the brindled cow started blinking to keep her eyes open. Then the girl said: 'Shall we go to sleep now?'

Once more the old man asked the creatures:

> 'Pretty cock, pretty hen,
> What say you then?
> Pretty brindled cow,
> What say you now?'

They answered 'Dux,

> 'With us you sat drinking
> And eating, and thinking
> Of us, as was right.
> We wish you good-night.'

Then she went upstairs, shook up the pillows, and put clean sheets on the beds, and when all was ready the old man came upstairs and got into bed, and his white beard came down to his feet.  The girl got into the other bed, said her prayers, and went to sleep.

She slept quietly until midnight, but then such a noise broke out in the house that she woke up.  There was such a cracking and rattling in the corners, and the doors burst open and slammed against the wall.  The beams groaned as if they would jump out of their mortises, and it seemed as if the stairs were falling down, and at last there was a loud crash as if the whole roof had collapsed.  When all was quiet again, and she saw there was no harm done, she stayed quietly in bed and went to sleep again.  But when in the morning she woke up to bright sunshine, what did she see?  She was lying in a great hall, and everything about her shone with royal splendour.  Green silk tapestries, worked with golden flowers, hung on the walls, her bedstead was of ivory, and the sheets of crimson satin, and on a chair beside it were a pair of slippers stitched with pearls. She thought it was a dream, but three richly clad servants came into the room and asked what was her command. 'Go away,' she answered. 'I 'm just going to get up and cook the old man some soup, and then I 'll feed the pretty cock and the hen, and the pretty brindled cow.'

She thought the old man must have got up already, and looked round for his bed. He was not in it, but a strange man lay there. As she was looking at him, noticing that he was young and handsome, he woke and sat up, saying: 'I am a prince, and an old witch put a spell on me, making me live as an old grey-bearded man alone in the forest, with no one by me but my three servants whom she turned into a cock and a hen and a brindled cow. The spell could not be broken until a young girl came to us who was good and kind, not only to men, but to beasts as well; and you were the one. Last night at midnight the spell was broken by you, and the old house in the forest was changed into my royal palace again.' When they had got up the king's son told the three servants to go away and fetch her father and mother to the wedding feast. 'But where are my sisters?' she asked. 'I shut them up in the cellar,' said he, 'and to-morrow they are to be led into the forest, to serve as maids in a charcoal-burner's house, until they have mended their ways and learnt not to let poor animals go hungry.'

# The Golden Bird

THE King of the East had a beautiful garden, and in the garden grew a tree that bore golden apples. These apples were always counted, but about the time when they began to grow ripe it was found that every night one of them was gone. The king was told this, and he ordered a watch to be kept under the tree all night.

The king set the eldest of his three sons to watch, but about twelve o'clock he fell asleep, and in the morning another of the apples was missing.

Then the second son was set to watch, and at midnight he too fell asleep, and in the morning another apple was gone.

Then the third son offered to keep watch: but the king

at first would not let him, for fear some harm should come to him. However, at last he yielded, and the young man laid himself under the tree to watch. As the clock struck twelve he heard a rustling noise in the air, and a bird came flying and sat upon the tree. This bird's feathers were all of pure gold, and as it was pecking at one of the apples with its beak the king's son jumped up and shot at it. The shot, however, did the bird no harm, it only dropped a golden feather from its tail, and flew away. The golden feather was then brought to the king in the morning, and all his council were called together. Every one agreed that it was the most beautiful thing that had ever been seen, and that it was worth more than all the wealth of the kingdom: but the king said: 'One feather is of no use to me, I must and will have the whole bird.'

Then the eldest son set out to find this golden bird, and thought to find it very easily; and when he had gone but a little way he came to a wood, and by the side of the wood he saw a fox sitting. The lad was fond of a little sport, so he took his gun and made ready to shoot at it. Then the fox cried out: 'Softly, softly! do not shoot me, I can give you good counsel. I know what your business is, and that you want to find the golden bird. You will reach a village in the evening, and when you get there you will see two inns, built one on each side of the street. The right-hand one is very pleasant and beautiful to look at, but go not in there. Rest for the night in the other, though it may seem to you very poor and mean.' 'What can such a stupid beast as this know about the matter?' thought the silly lad to himself. So he shot at the fox, but he missed it, and it only laughed at him, set up its tail above its back, and ran into the wood.

The young man went his way, and in the evening came

to the village where the two inns were. In the right-hand one people were singing and dancing and feasting; but the other looked very dirty and poor. 'I should be a fool indeed,' said he, 'if I went to that shabby house, and left this charming place.' So he went into the smart house, and ate and drank at his ease; and there he stayed, and forgot the bird and his father and his country too.

Time passed on, and as the eldest son did not come back, and no tidings were heard of him, the second son set out in search of the golden bird. He met with the fox sitting by the roadside, who gave him the same good advice as he had given his brother: but when he came to the two inns his eldest brother was standing at the window where the merry-making was, and called to him to come in; and he could not withstand the temptation, but went in, joined the merry-making, and lived only for pleasure.

Time passed on again, and the youngest son too wished to set out into the wide world, to seek for the golden bird; but his father would not listen to him, 'for,' said the king, 'it is of no use. He is no more likely to find the golden bird than his brothers were. And if he should meet with an accident he has not the sense to help himself.' However, at last it was agreed he should go; for, to tell the truth, he would not rest at home. As he came to the wood he met the fox, who begged for his life, and gave him the same good counsel that he had given the other brothers. But he spoke kindly to the fox, saying: 'Have no fear, little fox, I shall not harm you.' Then the fox said: 'Sit upon my tail, and you will travel faster.' So he sat down, and the fox began to run, and away they went over stock and stone so quickly that their hair whistled in the wind.

When they came to the village the young man got down and took the fox's advice; without looking about him he went straight to the shabby inn and rested there all night at his ease. In the morning came the fox again, and met him as he was beginning his journey, and said: 'Go straight forward until you come to a castle, before which lie a whole troop of soldiers fast asleep and snoring; take no notice of them, but go into the castle, and pass on and on till you come to a room where the golden bird sits in a wooden cage: close by it stands a beautiful golden cage; but do not try to take the bird out of the shabby cage and put it into the handsome one, otherwise you will be sorry for it.' Then the fox stretched out his brush again, and the young man sat himself down, and away they went over stock and stone till their hair whistled in the wind.

Before the castle gate all was as the fox had said: so the lad went in, and found the chamber, where the golden bird hung in a wooden cage. Below stood the golden cage; and the three golden apples that had been lost were lying about the room. Then he thought to himself: 'It would be ridiculous to bring away such a fine bird in this shabby cage'; so he opened the door and took hold of the bird, and put it into the golden cage. But it set up at once such a piercing scream that all the soldiers awoke; and they took him prisoner, and carried him off to prison.

The next morning the court sat to judge him; and as he confessed all, it doomed him to die unless he should bring the king the golden horse that could run as swiftly as the wind. If he did this he was to have the golden bird given him as a reward.

So he set out once more on his journey, sighing, and in great despair; when, on a sudden, he met his good friend the fox sitting in the road. 'Now you see,' said the fox, 'what has happened from your not listening to my advice. I will still, however, tell you how you may find the golden horse if you will but do as I bid you. You must go straight on till you come to the castle, where the horse stands in his stall. By his side will lie the groom fast asleep and snoring. Take away the horse softly, but be sure to let the old leathern saddle be upon him, and do not put on the golden one that is close by.' Then the young man sat down on the fox's tail, and away they went over stock and stone till their hair whistled in the wind.

All went right, and the groom lay snoring, with his hand upon the golden saddle. But when the lad looked at the horse he thought it would be an insult to such a fine beast not to put the good saddle on him.

But no sooner had the golden saddle touched his back than the horse began to neigh so loud that all the grooms ran in and took him prisoner; and in the morning he was brought before the king's court to be judged, and was at once doomed to die. But the king promised that if he could bring thither the beautiful princess from the golden castle he should live and have the horse given him for his own.

Then he went his way again very sorrowful; but the old fox once more met him on the road, and said: 'I ought to leave you to your fate. Yet I will once more give you counsel. Go straight on, and in the evening you will come to a castle. Every night when all is quiet the princess goes to the bath: go up to her as she passes and give her a kiss, and she will let you lead her away; but take care you do not let her go and take leave of her father and mother, or you will be sorry for it.' Then the fox stretched out his tail, and away they went over stock and stone till their hair whistled again.

As they came to the golden castle all was as the fox had said; and at twelve o'clock the young man met the princess going to the bath, and gave her a kiss; and she agreed to run away with him, but begged with many tears that he should let her take leave of her father. At first he said 'No,' but she wept still more and more, and fell at his feet, till at last he yielded; but the moment she came to her father's bed the guards awoke, and he was taken prisoner again.

So he was brought at once before the king, who lived in that castle. And the king said: 'Your life is forfeit unless in eight days you dig away the hill that stops the view from my window.'

The king's son shovelled and dug without respite, and when he had worked for seven days, and had done very little, he grew sad to see that all his work was in vain, and gave up hope. But the fox came and said: 'Lie down and go to sleep! I will work for you.' In the morning he awoke, and the hill was gone; so he went merrily to the king, and told him that now it was gone he must give him the princess.

The king was obliged to keep his word, and away went the young man and the princess. But the fox came again and said to him: 'You have done well. But the golden horse goes with the princess.' 'Ah!' said the young man, 'that would be a great thing; but how can it be?'

'If you will only listen,' said the fox, 'it can soon be done. When you come to the king of the castle where the golden horse is, and he asks for the beautiful princess, you must say: 'Here she is!' Then he will be very glad to see her, and will have the golden horse led out as a present to you, and you will mount and put out your hand to take leave of them; but shake hands with the princess last. When she grasps your hand lift her quickly on to the horse behind you, and gallop away as fast as you can. No one will be able to overtake you, for that horse is swifter than the wind.'

All went right; the king's son rode away on the golden

horse with the princess. The fox said: 'When you come to the castle where the bird is I will stay with the princess at the door, and you will ride in and speak to the king; and when he sees that it is the right horse he will bring out the bird: and when you get it into your hand ride back as fast as you can to us, and pick up the princess again.'

This, too, happened as the fox said.

As the king's son was about to ride home with the princess the fox said: 'Now you must reward me for my help.' 'What do you want?' asked the prince. 'Pray kill me, and cut off my head and my brush!' The young man would not do any such thing to so good a friend: so the fox said: 'Then we must part. I will at any rate give you good counsel: beware of two things: ransom no one from the gallows, and sit down on the rim of no well.' Then he went away. 'Well,' thought the young man, 'he's a strange beast! What fancies he has! Who would ransom people from the gallows! And as for sitting on the rim of a well, I never yet wanted to do it.'

So he rode on with the princess, till at last they came to the village where he had left his two brothers. And there he heard a great noise and uproar: and when he asked what was the matter the people said: 'Two rogues are going to be hanged.' As he came nearer he saw that the two men were his brothers, who had turned robbers. He asked: 'Can nothing save them from such a death?' But the people said: 'No! Unless you would bestow all your money upon the rascals, and buy their freedom. But why should you spend good money on wicked men.' Then he did not stay to think about it, but paid whatever was asked; and his brothers were given up, and went on with him towards their father's home.

Now the weather was very hot; and as they came to the

wood where the fox first met them they found it so cool and shady under the trees, beside a well, that the two brothers said: 'Let us sit down by the side of this well and rest awhile, to eat and drink.' 'Very good!' said he, and forgot what the fox had said, and sat down on the rim of the well: and while he thought no harm coming to him they pushed him down the well, and took the princess, the horse, and the bird, and went home to the king their father, and said: 'All these we have won by our own skill and strength.' Then there was great merriment made, and the king held a feast, and the two brothers were welcomed home; but the horse would not eat, the bird would not sing, and the princess sat by herself in her chamber, and wept bitterly.

But the youngest son was not dead. Luckily the well was nearly dry, and he fell in soft moss and took no harm, but he could find no way to get out. As he stood bewailing his fate, and thinking what he should do, to his great joy he spied his old and faithful friend the fox, looking down upon him. Then the fox scolded him for not following his advice, which would have saved him from all the troubles that had befallen him. 'Yet,' said he, 'silly as you have been, I cannot bear to leave you here; so lay hold of my brush, and hold fast!' Then he pulled him out of the well, and said to him, as he got out: 'You are not yet out of danger, your brothers were not sure you were dead, and have surrounded the wood with guards who are to kill you on sight.' So he changed clothes with a poor man who was sitting by the way, and came to the king's court. But he was scarcely within the gate when the horse began to eat, and the bird began to sing, and the princess left off weeping.

The king in amazement asked: 'What can this mean?' Then the maiden said: 'I know not how it is, but I was once so sad and now I feel so gay. It seems to me as if my true love had come back.' And she told him everything that had happened, although the other brothers had threatened to kill her if she should betray them. The king had all the people who were in the castle brought to his presence, and the young man in his old rags came with them. But the maiden recognized him, and fell on his neck. Then the wicked brothers were taken and put to death; but the third son was married to the princess, and made the king's heir.

But what became of the fox? A long time afterwards the king's son was walking in the wood when he met the fox, who said: 'Now you have all you can wish for, but there is no end to my misfortune, though it is in your power to set me free,' and again he besought him, with tears in his eyes, to be so kind as to cut off his head and his brush. At last he did so, though sorely against his will, and in the same moment the fox was changed into a prince, and the princess knew him to be her own brother, who had been lost a great many years; for a spiteful fairy had enchanted him with a spell that could only be broken by someone getting the golden bird, and by cutting off his head and his brush.

# The Twelve Huntsmen

THERE was once a king's son, who had a sweetheart,
and loved her much. Now as he was sitting con-
tentedly with her, news came to him that his father was
sick and likely to die, and had a great desire to see him
before his end came. So the prince said to his sweetheart:
'Now I must go away and leave you; keep this ring to
remember me by. When I am king I will come back and
fetch you home.' So he rode off, and when he got to his
father's house the king was very sick and near to death.

'Dear son,' he said, 'I wanted to see you once more before I died; promise me you will marry the one I shall name.' And he named the daughter of a certain king who was to be his wife.    The son was so sad that he took no thought what he was doing, but said: 'Yes, dear father, I will do as you wish.'    With that the king shut his eyes and died.

When the prince was proclaimed king, and the days of mourning were passed, he had to fulfil his promise that he had given to his father; so he sued for the hand of the king's daughter, and she consented.    When his old sweetheart heard that she nearly died of grief.    But her father said to her: 'Dear child, why are you so sad?    You shall have whatever you desire.'    She thought for a moment, and then said: 'Dear father, I want eleven maidens, exactly like me in face and form and stature.'    'If it is possible,' said the king, 'your wish shall be fulfilled.'    He had search made throughout his kingdom until eleven maidens were found, each like his daughter in face and form and stature.

When they were brought to the king's daughter she had twelve sets of huntsmen's clothing made, all alike, and the eleven maidens each put on a suit, and she put on the other one.    So she said good-bye to her father and rode off with them until she came to the court of her old sweetheart that she loved so much.    She asked if he were in need of huntsmen, and whether he would take them all into his service together.    The king looked at them without recognizing her, but because they were all such fine-looking young men he was glad to take them; so they became the twelve royal huntsmen.

Now the king had a lion, which was a wonderful animal, for it knew everything that was hidden and secret.    It happened one evening to say to the king: 'I suppose you think you have twelve huntsmen?'    'Why, yes,' said the king, 'twelve huntsmen they are.' 'You are wrong,' the lion went on, 'they are twelve maidens.' The king answered: 'That can never be true. How can you prove it?' 'Oh, just have some peas scattered about the floor of your ante-room,' answered the lion. 'You will soon see. Men have such a firm pace, that when they walk over peas none of the peas move. But girls go hopping and tripping and shuffling, so that the peas roll about.' The king was pleased with this advice, and he had the peas scattered.

But one of the king's servants was kind to the huntsmen, and when he heard that they were to be put to the test he went and told them everything, saying: 'The lion wishes to show the king that you are girls.' The king's daughter thanked him, and afterwards said to the maidens: 'Keep yourselves in hand, and tread firmly on the peas.' Next morning, when the king sent for the twelve huntsmen, they came into the ante-room where the peas were and trod firmly on them, walking so surely and sturdily that not one of the peas rolled about or so much as moved. They went out again, and the king said to the lion: 'You were lying to me. They walk like men.' The lion replied: 'They knew they would be put to the test, so they kept themselves in hand. But have twelve spinning-wheels brought into the antechamber, and when they pass them they will look at them with joy, as no man would do.' This notion pleased the king, and he had spinning-wheels put in the ante-room.

But the same servant who was friendly with the huntsmen went to them, and told them of the plot. When they were alone the king's daughter said to her eleven maidens: 'Control yourselves, and do not look at the spinning-wheels.' In the morning the king sent for his twelve huntsmen, and they came through the ante-room without looking at the spinning-wheels at all. Again the king said to the lion: 'You lied to me. They are men, for they never even looked at the spinning-wheels.' The lion answered: 'They knew they were being put to the test, and so they controlled themselves.' But the king had lost faith in the lion.

The twelve huntsmen attended the king regularly when he went hunting, and the longer they stayed the better he liked them. Now it came about that one day when they were hunting news was brought that the king's betrothed was approaching. When the rightful betrothed heard that she was so grieved that her heart almost ceased to beat, and she fell to the ground in a faint. The king thought his favourite huntsman had had an accident, so he ran to the spot to help him, and pulled off his glove. Then he saw the ring which he had given to his first sweetheart, and when he looked at her face he recognized her. His heart was so touched that he kissed her, and when she opened her eyes he said: 'You are mine and I am yours, and no one in all the world can alter that.' But he sent a message to his second sweetheart, asking her to go back to her own country because he had a wife already, and he who finds the old key does not need a new one. So the wedding-feast was held; and the lion was taken back into favour, for he had spoken the truth after all.

# The White Snake

LONG ago there lived a king whose wisdom was re-
nowned throughout the whole country. There was
nothing he did not know, and it seemed as if news of the
most hidden things was borne to him through the air. But
he had a strange habit. Every day at noon, when the table
was cleared and no one else remained at it, a trusted servant
was charged to bring in another dish. It was covered,

and the servant himself did not know what was under the lid, nor did any man else, for the king never took the lid off nor ate out of it until he was quite alone.   This lasted a long time, until one day curiosity overcame the servant who was taking the dish away; he could not resist taking the dish up to his room.   When he had carefully locked the door he lifted the lid and saw a white snake in the dish. As soon as he saw it he could not help tasting it; he cut off a piece and put it in his mouth.   No sooner had it touched his tongue than he heard outside his window a queer whispering of thin voices.   He went and listened, and then he understood it was the sparrows, talking together and telling each other what was going on in the fields and the woods.   Tasting the snake had given him the power of understanding the speech of beasts.

Now it so happened that on that very day the queen mislaid her finest ring and suspicion fell on the trusted servant, who had access to the whole palace, of having stolen it.   The king summoned him to his presence, and threatened him with much abuse, that if by the next day he could not name the thief he would be held guilty and put to death.   It was of no avail for him to proclaim his innocence, and he was taken away without getting better terms. Full of fear and disquiet he went down into the courtyard and considered how he could get out of his scrape.   Some ducks were sitting by a running stream, resting and smoothing their feathers with their beaks as they held a private conversation.   The servant stopped and listened to them. They were saying where they had been waddling about all the morning, and what sort of food they had found.   One of them said rather peevishly: 'I have a ring lying heavy on my stomach, which I gulped down this morning under the queen's window, I was in such a hurry.'   The servant seized the duck by the neck and carried her into the kitchen. He said to the cook: 'Kill this one, she's fat enough by now.' 'Why, yes,' said the cook, weighing her in his hand, 'she's gone to some trouble to put on weight, and has been ready for the pot a long time.' He cut off her head, and when they had drawn her the queen's ring was found in her gizzard. Now the servant was easily able to prove his innocence to the king, who, in order to make good the wrong done him, promised to grant him a boon and offered him the most honourable position at court that he could wish.

The servant asked for no more than a horse and travelling money, for he had a great wish to see the world, and travel about in it a little. When his wish was granted he set off, and one day was riding past a pond when he noticed three fish that had got stuck in the rushes and were gasping for water. Although people say 'As dumb as a fish,' he could understand their speech, and how they were lamenting their miserable end. Because he had pity on them, he got off his horse, and put the three trapped fishes back in the water. They splashed about joyfully, stuck their heads out of the water, and called to him: 'We shall remember you and reward you for saving us.' He rode on, and after a while heard something like a voice in the sand at his feet. He listened, and heard the king of the ants complaining: 'If only men would leave us alone with their great beasts! That stupid horse is trampling my people to death with his heavy hoofs!' He turned aside on to another path, and the king of the ants called to him: 'We shall remember you and reward you.' The road led into a forest, and there he saw a pair of ravens standing beside their nest and throwing their children out of it. 'Away with you, gallows chicks,' they cried, 'we can feed you no more; now you are big enough to forage for yourselves.' The poor young ravens lay on the ground, fluttering and beating their wings, and crying: 'We poor helpless children, how are we to feed ourselves when we cannot yet fly? What is there left for us but to die of hunger here?' Then the kind youth dismounted, killed his horse with his sword, and left it for the young ravens to feed on. They hopped up to it, ate their fill, and called after him: 'We shall remember you and reward you.'

Now he had to go on foot, and when he had walked a long way he came to a great city. There was much noise and jostling in the streets, and presently a man on horseback came and cried aloud: 'The king's daughter is seeking a husband, but the man who would woo her must perform a difficult task, and if he cannot do it his life is forfeit.' Now many had attempted this and lost their lives in vain. The youth, when he saw the king's daughter, was so blinded by her beauty that he forgot all about the danger, and went to the king to present himself as a suitor.

Immediately he was led out to the seashore, and before his eyes a golden ring was thrown into the water. Then the king commanded him to fetch the ring up again from the bottom of the sea, and added: 'If you come up without it, then you will be thrown back into the water again and again until you perish in the waves.' Every one was sorry for the young man, and left him alone by the sea.

He stood on the shore thinking what he should do, when all at once he saw three fishes swimming towards him, and who should they be but the three whose lives he had saved. The middle one held a mussel in his mouth, which he laid on the shore at the feet of the young man, and when he lifted it up and opened it there was the ring inside. With joy he brought it to the king, expecting to be given the promised reward. But when the proud king's daughter perceived that he was not as high-born as she, she scorned him, and demanded that he should perform a second task. She went down into the garden and strewed ten sacks full of millet on the grass with her own hand. 'Before the sun rises in the morning,' she said, 'you must pick it all up. And not a seed must be missing.'

The young man sat down in the garden, thinking how he could possibly perform this task, but he could think of no way to do it, so sat gloomily awaiting the morning, when he should be led to death. But when the first rays of the sun peeped into the garden he saw the ten sacks standing side by side, full of millet, and not a grain missing. For the king of the ants had come in the night with thousands and thousands of ants, and the grateful creatures had gathered together with care all the millet and put it in the sacks. The king's daughter came down into the garden herself and was astonished to see that the young man had done what she had set him to do. But she could not yet overcome her hard heart, and said: 'Even if he has performed both these tasks he shall not marry me until he has brought me an apple from the tree of life.'

The young man did not know where to find the tree of life; he got up and was ready to keep on searching as long as his legs would carry him, but had no hope of finding it. By the time he had wandered through three kingdoms he came to a forest, and sat down under a tree to sleep. Then he heard a rustling in the branches, and a golden apple fell into his hand. At the same time three ravens flew down down to him, perched on his knee, and said: 'We are the three young ravens whom you saved from starving to death. Now we are grown up and have heard that you were looking for the golden apple. So we flew across the sea to the end of the world, where the tree of life grows, and we fetched the apple.' Joyfully the young man set off home, and brought the golden apple to the king's beautiful daughter, who could now no longer put off matters. They halved the apple of life, and ate it together: then her heart was filled with love for him, and they lived together to a ripe old age in undisturbed happiness.

## Little Red Riding Hood

ONCE upon a time there was a dear little girl who was liked by every one who met her, but especially by her grandmother, who would have given her anything. Once she gave her a little hood of red satin, that suited her so well that she refused to wear anything instead of it; and so she was called Red Riding Hood. One day her mother said to her: 'Now, Red Riding Hood, here is a piece of cake and a bottle of wine to take to your grandmother's; she is very ill and weak, and it will do her good. Set off before it gets too hot, and when you get out into the country mind you go carefully, and don't stray away from the path, or you might fall and break the bottle, and then your granny wouldn't get any. And when you get to her house remember to say "Good morning" first, and don't begin by peering into all the corners.'

'I 'll be good all right,' said Red Riding Hood, and gave her mother her hand on it. Now her grandmother lived out in the forest, half an hour's walk from the village. As soon as Red Riding Hood got into the forest she met the wolf. But Red Riding Hood did not know what a wicked beast he was, and she was not afraid of him.

'Good morning, Red Riding Hood,' said he.

'Good morning, wolf.'

'Whither away so early, Red Riding Hood?'

'To see granny.'

'What have you got under your apron?'

'Cakes and wine. Yesterday was baking day. Granny is weak and ill, and this will do her good and make her strong.'

'Red Riding Hood, where does your grandmother live?'

'About another quarter of an hour's walk further into the wood, under the three big oak-trees. Her house is just above the nut-bushes, you must know it,' said Red Riding Hood.

The wolf thought to himself: 'How young and tender she is, she will make a tasty morsel, even nicer than the old woman; you must set about this cunningly if you want to eat up both of them.' So he walked along with Red Riding Hood a little way, and then he said: 'Red Riding Hood, look at the pretty flowers all round us; why don't you have a look round? Can't you hear how sweetly the birds are singing? You walk straight ahead as if you were going to school, and yet it 's such fun out here in the forest.'

Red Riding Hood looked up, and when she saw the sunbeams dancing to and fro among the trees, and the beautiful flowers all around her, she thought: 'If I fetch granny a bunch of flowers it will make her happy. It 's so early now, I shall have plenty of time.' She ran off the path into the forest, looking for flowers. No sooner had she picked one than it seemed to her that there was a finer one a little farther off, and so she went after it, and got deeper and deeper into the forest. But the wolf went straight on to her grandmother's house, and knocked on the door.

'Who 's there?'

'Red Riding Hood, with cake and wine. Open the door.'

'Just pull the latch,' said the grandmother. 'I am too weak to get up.'

The wolf pulled the latch, the door opened, and without saying a word he went straight up to grandmother's bed-side and ate her up. Then he put on her clothes, pulled her nightcap on to his head, and got into bed, pulling the bed-curtains round him.

Now Red Riding Hood had been running about looking for flowers, and when she had gathered so many that she could not carry any more, she began to think of her grand-mother again, and set off for her house. She was surprised to find the door left open; everything seemed so strange that she thought: 'Oh dear, how frightened I am to-day, and yet usually I do so enjoy visiting granny.' She called 'Good morning,' but there was no answer. So she went to the bed and pulled the curtains back; there lay her grandmother with her nightcap pulled over her ears and looking very strange.

'Oh, granny, what big ears you have!'

'All the better to hear you with.'

'Oh, granny, what big eyes you have!'

'All the better to see you with.'

'Oh, granny, what big hands you have!'

'All the better to grab you with.'

'But granny, what a horrible great mouth you have!'

'All the better to eat you with.'

No sooner had the wolf said this than he made one pounce out of bed and ate poor Red Riding Hood up.

When the wolf had satisfied his appetite he got back into bed, fell asleep, and began to snore much too loud. The gamekeeper was just walking past the house and thought: 'How the old lady snores! I must go and see if she is all right.' So he went into the bedroom, and when he got in front of the bed he saw the wolf lying there.

'So there you are, you old sinner,' he said. 'I've been looking for you for a long time.' He was just going to aim his gun at him when he thought the wolf might have eaten the old lady up, and if he shot him he would not be able to save her. So he did not shoot, but found a pair of scissors, and cut the wolf open as he slept. When he had made a snip or two he saw the glint of the red riding hood, and out jumped the little girl after a few more snips, crying: 'Oh, how frightened I was! It was so dark inside the wolf!' They got the old lady out alive too, but she could hardly breathe. Now Red Riding Hood hurried out and fetched some big stones, and they filled up the wolf's inside with them, and when he woke up he tried to run away, but the stones were too heavy for him, and he soon tottered and fell down dead.

Then they were all happy. The gamekeeper skinned the wolf and took the skin home with him; the grandmother ate the cakes and drank the wine which Red Riding Hood had brought her, and felt better. But Red Riding Hood thought: 'For the rest of your life you will never wander off into the forest again, when your mother has told you to keep to the path.'

# The Singing Jark

A MERCHANT, who had three daughters, was once
setting out upon a journey; but before he went he
asked each daughter what gift he should bring back for
her. The eldest wished for pearls; the second for jewels;

but the third, who was called Lily, said: 'Dear father, bring me back a singing, soaring lark.' Her father said he would try what he could do. So he kissed all three and bid them good-bye.

And when the time came for him to go home he had bought pearls and jewels for the two eldest, but he sought everywhere in vain for the singing, soaring lark, though he had searched everywhere.

This grieved him very much, for Lily was his dearest child; and as he was journeying home, thinking what he should bring her, he came to a fine castle; and beside the castle grew a tree, and on top of the tree sat a lark singing away. 'Just in time,' he said, and ordered his servant to climb and catch the bird.

No sooner had he got near the tree than up sprang a fierce lion, and roared out: 'Whoever steals my lark shall be eaten alive!' Then the man said: 'I knew not that the lark belonged to you, I will make good the damage, and pay much money as ransom, if only you will spare my life.' 'No!' said the lion, 'nothing can save you unless you undertake to give me whatever meets you first on your return home: if you agree to this I will give you your life, and the lark, too, for your daughter.' But the man was unwilling to do so, and said: 'It may be my youngest daughter, who loves me most, and always runs to meet me when I go home.' Then the servant was greatly frightened, and said: 'It may perhaps be only a cat or a dog.' And at last the man yielded with a heavy heart, and took the lark; and said he would give the lion whatever should meet him first on his return.

And as he came near home it was Lily, his youngest and dearest daughter, that met him; and she came running and kissed him, and welcomed him home; and when she saw that he had brought her the lark she was still more glad. But her father began to be very sorrowful and to weep, saying: 'Alas, my dearest child! I have bought this bird at a high price, for I have said I would give you to a wild lion; and when he has you he will tear you to pieces, and eat you.' Then he told her all that had happened, and said she should not go, let what would happen.

But she comforted him and said: 'Dear father, the word you have given must be kept; I will go to the lion and soothe him: perhaps he will let me come safe home again.'

The next morning she asked the way she was to go, and took leave of her father, and went forth with a bold heart into the wood. But the lion was an enchanted prince. By day he and all his court were lions, but in the evening they took their right forms again. And when Lily came to the castle, he welcomed her so courteously that she agreed to marry him. The wedding feast was held, and they lived happily together a long time. The prince was only to be seen as soon as evening came, and then he held his court; but every morning he left his bride, and went away by himself, she knew not whither, till the night came again.

After some time he said to her: 'To-morrow there will be a great feast in your father's house, for your eldest sister is to be married; and if you wish to go and visit her my lions shall lead you thither.' Then she rejoiced much at the thoughts of seeing her father once more, and set out with the lions; and every one was overjoyed to see her, for they had thought her dead long since. But she told them how happy she was, and stayed till the feast was over, and then went back to the wood.

Her second sister was soon after married, and when Lily was asked to the wedding she said to the prince: 'I will not go alone this time—you must go with me.' But he would not, and said that it would be a very hazardous thing, for if the least ray of the torchlight should fall upon him his enchantment would become still worse, for he should be changed into a dove, and be forced to wander about the world for seven long years. However, she gave him no rest, and said she would take care no light should fall upon him. So at last they set out together, and took with them their little child, and she chose a large hall with thick walls for him to sit in while the wedding torches were lighted; but unluckily, no one saw that the door was made of unseasoned wood, which warped and had a crack in it. Then the wedding feast was held with great pomp, but as the procession came from the church, and passed with the torches before the hall, a very small ray of light fell upon the prince. In a moment he disappeared, and when his wife came in and looked for him she found only a white dove; and it said to her: 'Seven years must I fly up and down over the face of the earth, but every seven paces I will let fall a drop of blood and a white feather, that will show you the way I am going; follow it, and at last you may overtake me and set me free.'

This said, he flew out at the door, and poor Lily followed; and every seven paces a white feather fell and a drop of blood, and showed her the way she was to journey. Thus she went roving on through the wide world, and looked neither to the right hand nor to the left, nor took any rest, for seven years. Then she began to be glad, and thought to herself that the time was fast coming when all her troubles should end; yet repose was still far off, for one day as she was travelling on she missed the white feather, and when she lifted up her eyes she could nowhere see the dove. 'Now,' thought she to herself, 'no aid of man can be of use to me.' So she went to the sun and said: 'Thou shinest everywhere, on the hill's top and the valley's depth—hast thou anywhere seen my white dove?' 'No,' said the sun, 'I have not seen it; but I will give thee a casket—open it when thine hour of need comes.'

So she thanked the sun, and went on her way till eventide; and when the moon arose she cried up to it, and said: 'Thou shinest through all the night, over field and grove; hast thou nowhere seen my white dove?' 'No,' said the moon, 'I cannot help thee; but I will give thee an egg— break it when need comes.'

Then she thanked the moon, and went on till the night wind blew; and she raised up her voice to it, and said: 'Thou blowest through every tree and under every leaf: hast thou not seen my white dove?' 'No,' said the night wind, 'but I will ask the three other winds; perhaps they have seen it.' Then the east wind and the west wind came, and said they too had not seen it, but the south wind said: 'I have seen the white dove—he has flown to the Red Sea, and is changed once more into a lion, for the seven years are passed away, and there he is fighting with a dragon; and the dragon is an enchanted princess, who seeks to separate him from thee.' Then the night wind said: 'I will give thee counsel. Go to the Red Sea; on the right shore stand many rods—count them, and when thou comest to the eleventh, break it off, and smite the dragon with it; and so the lion will have the victory, and both of them will appear to thee in their own forms. Then look round and thou wilt see a griffin, winged like a bird, sitting by the Red Sea; jump on his back with thy beloved one as quickly as possible, and he will carry you over the waters to your home. I will also give thee this nut,' continued the night wind. 'When thou art half-way over throw it down, and out of the waters will immediately spring up a high nut-tree, on which the griffin will be able to rest, otherwise he would not have the strength to bear you the whole way; if, therefore, thou dost forget to throw down the nut, he will drop you both into the sea.'

So the poor wanderer went forth, and found all as the night wind had said; and she plucked the eleventh rod, and smote the dragon, and the lion forthwith became a prince, and the dragon a princess again. But no sooner was the princess released from the spell than she seized the prince by the arm and sprang on to the griffin's back, and went off carrying the prince away with her.

Thus the unhappy maiden was again forsaken and forlorn; but she took heart and said: 'As far as the wind blows, and so long as the cock crows, I will journey on, till I find him once again.' She went on for a long long way, till at length she came to the castle whither the princess had carried the prince; and there was a feast got ready, and she heard that a wedding was about to be held. 'Heaven aid me now!' said she, and she took the casket that the sun had given her, and found that within it lay a dress as dazzling as the sun itself. So she put it on and went into the palace, and all the people gazed at her; and the dress pleased the princess so much that she asked whether it was to be sold. 'Not for gold or silver,' said she, 'but for flesh and blood.' The princess asked what she meant, and she said: 'Let me speak with the bridegroom this night in his chamber, and I will give thee the dress.' At last the princess agreed, but she told the chamberlain to give the prince a sleeping draught, that he might not hear or see her. When evening came, and the prince had fallen asleep, she was led to his chamber, and she sat herself down at his feet and said: 'I have followed thee seven years, I have been to the sun, the moon, and the night-wind, to seek thee, and at last I have helped thee to overcome the dragon. Wilt thou forget me quite?' But the prince all the time slept so soundly that her voice only passed over him, and seemed like the whistling of the wind among the fir trees.

Then poor Lily was led away, and forced to give up the golden dress; and when she saw that there was no help for her she went out into a meadow and sat herself down and wept. But as she sat she bethought herself of the egg that the moon had given her; and when she broke it there ran out a hen and twelve chickens of pure gold, that played about, and then nestled under the old one's wings, so as to form the most beautiful sight in the world. And she rose up and drove them before her, till the bride saw them from the window, and was so pleased that she came forth and asked her if she would sell the brood. 'Not for gold or silver, but for flesh and blood: let me again this evening speak with the bridegroom in his chamber, and I will give you the whole brood.'

Then the princess thought to betray her as before, and agreed to what she asked: but when the prince went to his chamber he asked the chamberlain why the wind had whistled so in the night. And the chamberlain told him all—how he had had to give him a sleeping draught, because a poor maiden had been sleeping in his room, and was to come again that night. Then the prince took care to throw away the sleeping draught: and when Lily came and began again to tell him what woes had befallen her, and how faithful and true she had been to him, he knew his beloved wife's voice, and sprang up and said: 'Only now am I released. I have been as if in a dream, for the strange princess had thrown a spell around me, so that I had altogether forgotten you; but Heaven has taken this madness from me in time.'

And they stole away out of the palace by night unawares, for they were afraid of the princess's father, who was a wizard, and seated themselves on the griffin, who flew back with them over the Red Sea. When they were half-way across Lily let the nut fall into the water and immediately a large nut-tree arose from the sea, whereon the griffin rested for a while, and then carried them safely home. There they found their child now grown up to be comely and fair: and after all their troubles they lived happily together to the end of their days.

# The Brave Little Tailor

ONE summer morning a little tailor was sitting on his table by the window, sewing merrily away for dear life, when a countrywoman came down the street crying: 'Good jam for sale! Good jam for sale!' The little tailor pricked up his ears and stuck his head out of the window calling: 'Come up here, madam, I'll buy your wares.' The woman came up three flights of stairs with her heavy basket on her arm, and he asked her to put out all her jars for him to choose from. He looked at them all, held them up to the light, sniffed them, and said at last: 'It seems good jam to me: weigh me out four ounces, madam, and if it comes to a quarter of a pound I don't care.'

The woman, who had hoped to make a good sale, gave him what he asked for, but went away grumbling angrily. 'Now may the Lord bless this jam, and let it give me strength and courage,' cried the tailor, fetching bread from the cupboard, and cutting off a whole round, which he spread with jam. 'It will taste sweet,' he thought. 'But first I will finish this doublet, before I taste it.' He put the slice of bread down beside him and went on sewing, making bigger and bigger stitches in his joy. Meanwhile the smell of jam rose up to the crowds of flies that were clinging to the wall, till it tempted them down to settle on the jam in swarms. 'Hey, who asked you to eat my jam?' said the little tailor, and chased them away. But the flies, who did not understand his speech, would not be put off, but came back in greater numbers than ever. This was too much for the little tailor; he reached for a rag, and shouting: 'I 'll show you!' he brought it down on top of them. When he lifted up the rag there were no fewer than seven dead flies, with their feet in the air. 'What a fellow you are!' he cried, for he had to admire his own bravery. 'The whole town shall hear of this.' And quickly he cut himself out a girdle, sewed it, and stitched on it in great letters: 'Seven at One Blow.' 'Town, indeed!' he went on, 'the whole world shall know of it!' and his heart leapt for joy like a lamb in spring.

The tailor, who was a very little man, bound his girdle round his body, and prepared to sally forth into the wide world, for he now considered his workshop too small for his valour, and looked about his house to see if there was anything good that he could take with him on his journey into the wide world. He could only find an old cheese; but that was better than nothing, so he took it off the shelf; and as he went out he found a bird caught in a bush; he stuffed that into his wallet with the cheese.

Then off he set, and as he climbed a high hill he saw a giant sitting on the top, who looked down upon him with a friendly smile. 'Good day, comrade,' said the tailor;

'there you sit at your ease like a gentleman, looking the wide world over; I have a mind to go and try my luck in that same world. What do you say to going with me?' Then the giant looked down, turned up his nose at him, and said: 'You are a poor trumpery little knave!' 'That may be,' said the tailor; 'but read this, and see what sort of man I am!'

The giant reading 'Seven at One Blow' thought that they had been men that the tailor had slain, and began to be somewhat more respectful; so he said: 'Very well, we shall soon see who is to be master.' He took up a large stone in his hand, and squeezed it till water dropped from it. 'Do that,' said he, 'if you have a mind to be thought a strong man.' 'Is that all?' said the tailor; 'I will soon do as much.' So he put his hand into his wallet, pulled out of it the cheese, and squeezed it till the whey ran out. 'What do you say now, Mr. Giant? My squeeze was a better one than yours.' Then the giant, not seeing that it was only a cheese, did not know what to say for himself, though he could hardly believe his eyes. At last he took up a stone, and threw it up so high that it went almost out of sight. 'Now then, little pigmy, do that if you can.' 'Very good,' said the other; 'your throw was not a bad one, but after all your stone fell to the ground; I will throw something that shall not fall at all.' 'That you can't do,' said the giant. But the tailor took out of the wallet the bird, and threw her up in the air; and she, pleased enough to be set free, flew away out of sight. 'Now, comrade,' said he, 'what do you say to that?' 'I will say you certainly can throw,' said the giant; 'but we will now try how you can work.'

Then he led him into the wood where a fine oak-tree lay felled. 'Come, let us drag it out of the wood together, if you are strong enough.' 'Oh, very well,' said the tailor; 'do you take hold of the trunk, and I will carry all the top

and the branches, which are much the largest and heaviest.'
So the giant took the trunk and laid it on his shoulder; but
the tailor sprang up and sat himself at his ease among the
branches, and so let the giant, who could not look round,
carry stem, branches, and tailor into the bargain. All the
way they went he made merry, and whistled and sang his
song: 'There were three tailors rode out of town,' as if
carrying the tree were mere sport; while the giant, after he
had borne it a good way, could carry it no longer, and said:
'I must let it fall.' Then the tailor sprang down, and held
the tree as if he were carrying it, saying: 'What a shame
that such a big fellow as you cannot even carry a tree.'

On they went together till they came to a tall cherry-
tree; the giant took hold of the top branch, and bent it down
to pluck the ripest fruit, and when he had done gave it over
to his friend, that he too might eat. But the little man
was so weak that he could not hold the tree, and up he went
with it, dangling in the air. 'Hallo!' said the giant, 'what
now? can't you hold that twig?' 'To be sure I could,'
said the other, who had fallen down without hurting himself. 'What is that to a man who has killed "Seven at One
Blow"? But don't you see that sportsman who is going
to shoot into the bush where we stood? I took a jump over
the tree to be out of his way: you had better do the same.'
The giant tried to follow, but the tree was far too high to
jump over, and he only stuck fast in the branches, for the
tailor to laugh at him. 'Well, you are a fine fellow after
all,' said the giant; 'so come home and sleep with me and
a friend of mine in our cave to-night, we will give you a hot
supper and a good bed.'

The tailor, who had no business upon his hands, accepted
the invitation. When they got to the cave more giants
were sitting round the fire, each with a whole roast sheep

in his hand.    The tailor looked round and thought: 'This is a good deal more spacious than my shop.'

The giant showed him a bed and invited him to lie down and sleep; but the tailor found the bed too big to lie down upon, and crept into a corner and there slept soundly. When midnight came the giant stepped softly in with his iron walking-stick, and gave such a stroke upon the bed, where he thought his guest was lying, that he said to himself: 'It 's all up with that grasshopper now; I shall have no more of his tricks.'

In the morning the giants went off into the woods, and quite forgot the tailor, till on a sudden they met him trudging along, whistling a merry tune; and so frightened were they at the sight, that they ran away as fast as they could.

Then on went the little tailor, following his pointed nose, till at last he reached the grounds of the king's palace.    And since he was tired he lay down on the grass and went to sleep.    While he was lying there the people of that country came and looked him up and down, and read the lettering on his girdle: 'Seven at One Blow.'    'Ah,' they cried, 'what is such a mighty man of war doing here in peace-time?    He must indeed be a great and powerful lord.' They went and told the king that there was an important and useful man, whose services would be worth any money if war should break out.    The king was pleased with this advice, and sent one of his courtiers to stand by the tailor until he should wake up, when he was to offer to take him into the king's service.    The messenger waited beside him until he began to stretch his limbs and open his eyes, and then made the offer.    'That is just what I came for,' answered the tailor, 'I am ready to enter the service of the king.'    So he was worthily received and given lodgings to himself.

But the soldiers were uncomfortable in his presence, and wished him a thousand miles away. 'What will happen,' they asked, 'if we should fall out with him, and he attacks us? He would kill seven of us at a time. That would be too much for us.' So they resolved to go to the king and give him notice. 'We cannot bear to serve with a man,' they said, 'who can kill seven at one blow.' The king was sorry to lose all his soldiers for the sake of one man, and wished he had never set eyes on him, and could get rid of him. But he dared not discharge him, for fear he would kill him and all his people, and set himself on the throne. He thought and thought, and at last hit on a plan. He sent for the little tailor to say that as he was such a great warrior he would make him an offer.

Two giants, who lived in a part of the kingdom a long way off, were become the dread of the whole land; for they had begun to rob, plunder, and ravage all about them. If he were so great a man as he said he should have a hundred soldiers, and should set out to fight these giants; and if he beat them he should have his daughter to wife and half the kingdom. 'With all my heart!' said he; 'but as for your hundred soldiers, I believe I shall do as well without them. A man that has killed seven at one blow need not quail before two.'

However they set off together, till they came to a wood. 'Wait here, my friends,' said he to the soldiers. 'I will soon give a good account of these giants'; and on he went, casting his sharp little eyes here, there, and everywhere around him. After a while he spied them both lying under a tree, and snoring away, till the very boughs bent up and down with the breeze.

The little man filled his wallet with stones and climbed up into the tree under which the giants lay.

As soon as he was safely up he threw one stone after another at the nearest giant, till at last he woke up in a rage, and shook his companion, crying out: 'What did you strike me for?' 'Nonsense, you are dreaming,' said the other, 'I did not strike you.' Then they both lay down to sleep again, and the tailor threw a stone at the second giant, which hit him on the tip of his nose. Up he sprang, and cried: 'What are you about? you struck me.' 'I did not,' said the other; and on they wrangled for a while, till, as both were tired, they made up the matter and fell asleep again. But then the tailor began his game once more, and flung the largest stone he had in his wallet with all his force, and hit the first giant in the eye. 'That is too bad,' cried he, roaring as if he was mad, 'I will not bear it.' So he pushed the other against the tree so that it shook. He, of course, was not pleased with this, and paid him back in kind, and at last a bloody battle began; up flew the trees by the roots, the rocks and stones were sent bang at one another's head, and in the end both lay dead upon the spot.

'It is a good thing,' said the tailor, 'that they let my tree stand, or I would have had to jump like a squirrel.'

Then down he ran, and took his sword, and gave each of them two or three very deep wounds on the breast, and set off to look for the soldiers.

'There lie the giants,' said he, 'I have killed them: but it was no small job, for they even tore trees up in their struggle. But they stood no chance against a man like me, that can kill seven at one blow.' 'Have you any wounds?' asked they. 'Wounds! that is a likely matter truly,' said he; 'they could not touch a hair of my head.' But the soldiers would not believe him till they rode into the wood, and found the giants weltering in their blood, and the trees lying around torn up by the roots.

The tailor claimed his promised reward from the king, who repented of his bargain, and cast about for a means of getting rid of his hero. So he said: 'You have not done yet; there is a unicorn running wild about the neighbouring woods, and doing a great deal of damage, and before I give you my daughter you must go after it and catch it, and bring it to me here alive.'

'After two giants I shall not have much fear for a unicorn. Seven at one blow, that's my style!' said the tailor, and he started off, carrying with him an axe and a rope.

On reaching the wood he bade his followers wait on the outskirts while he went in by himself. It was not long before the unicorn came in sight and forthwith made a rush for the tailor, as if to run him through without more ado.

'Not quite so fast, not quite so fast,' cried the little man, 'gently does it,' and he stood still until the animal was nearly upon him, and then sprang nimbly behind a tree.

The unicorn now made a fierce leap towards the tree, and drove his horn into the trunk with such violence that he had not the strength to pull it out again, and so he remained caught.

'I have him safely now,' said the tailor, and coming forward from behind the tree he put the rope round the animal's neck, cut the horn out of the tree with his axe, and led him captive before the king.

The king was unwilling to give him the reward he had promised, and challenged him a third time. Before the wedding the tailor was to capture a wild boar that was doing much harm in his forests, and the royal huntsmen were to help him. 'I will gladly do it,' said the tailor, 'it is child's play to me.' He did not take the huntsmen into the forest with him, at which they were pleased enough, because the boar had already given them such a reception that they had no stomach for another encounter. When the boar saw the tailor it rushed at him foaming at the mouth, and gnashing its tusks, ready to throw him to the ground. But the nimble champion sprang into an old chapel that stood in the wood, and with one bound he jumped out again by a window. The boar rushed in after him, but he ran round quickly and slammed the door behind it. Now the raging beast was caught, being too heavy and clumsy to jump out of the window. The little tailor called to the huntsmen to come and see the trapped boar, while he went straight to the king, who had no other choice but to fulfil his promise, and give him his daughter's hand and half his kingdom. Had he known that he had to deal with a tailor, and not with a great warrior, he would have been even less willing. So the wedding was held with great splendour and little joy, and the tailor became king.

After a while the young queen heard her husband cry out in his sleep: 'Now, boy, finish the jerkin and sew up the hose, or you 'll have my yardstick about your ears.' So she guessed where her young lord had been brought up, and in the morning she told her father her trouble, and asked him to get rid of this husband who was nothing but a tailor. The king comforted her with these words: 'Leave the door of your room open to-night. I will post my servants outside, and when he is asleep they shall go in and bind him and carry him off to a ship that will sail away with him to the other end of the earth.' She was content with that, but the king's squire, who overheard their plot, was friendly to the young lord and told him all.

'I'll put a spoke in their wheel,' said the tailor. That night he went to bed at the usual time; when his wife thought he was asleep she got up, opened the door, and went back to bed. The little tailor, who had only pretended to be asleep, began to cry out loud and clear: 'Boy, finish that jerkin and patch those breeches, or you'll have my yard-stick about your ears. I have killed seven at one blow, slain two giants, taken the unicorn alive, and captured the great wild boar. Do you think I am afraid of those who are now waiting outside the door?' When they heard this fear overcame them, and they ran as if a pack of fiends were after them, and no one dared lay a finger on him. And so the little tailor became king and remained so all his life.

# Rapunzel

THERE were once a man and his wife who had long wished in vain for a child, until at last it seemed that their wish would come true. At the back of their house was a little window which looked out on to a splendid garden, full of the most beautiful flowers and vegetables; but there was a high wall all round it and no one dared go inside because it belonged to a witch of great power whom everybody feared. One day the wife was standing at her window, looking down into the garden, when she saw a bed planted with the most lovely rampions. They looked so fresh and green that she began to hanker after some of them to eat. The hankering grew stronger every day, and when she knew that she could get none of them to eat she began to pine away and look pale and poorly. Her husband was frightened, and asked: 'What is the matter, dear?' 'Ah,' she said, 'if I don't get some of the rampions out of the garden behind our house to eat I shall die.'

The man, who loved her, thought to himself: 'Rather than let your wife die you must get her some of those rampions, come what may.' So in the twilight he climbed over the wall of the witch's garden, hastily grabbed a handful of rampions, and took them to his wife. She made them into a salad straight away, and ate them with relish. But she enjoyed them so very much that the next day her longing for them was three times as great. She would not be content; her husband must once more climb over the garden wall. So he went down there again, but when he had got over the wall he was terrified to see the witch standing in front of him.

'How dare you,' she said, giving him an angry look, 'climb into my garden and steal my rampions from me like a thief? You shall be sorry for it.' 'Oh,' he said, 'have pity on me, for it was need drove me to it. My wife saw your rampions out of the window, and she has such a longing for them she would die if she could not get some of them to eat.' Then the witch became less angry, and said: 'If things are as you say, then you may take away as many rampions as you wish, but on one condition: you must give me the child that is going to be born. All shall go well with it, and I shall care for it like a mother.' In his fear the husband agreed to all this, and as soon as the baby was born the witch appeared, named the child 'Rapunzel' (for that was what people called rampions in that country), and took it away.

Rapunzel grew into the prettiest little girl under the sun. When she was twelve the witch shut her up in a tower that lay in the midst of a dark wood, and had no door and no stairs, only a little window high up at the top. When the witch wanted to go up she stood at the foot of the tower and cried:

> 'Rapunzel Rapunzel,
> Let down your hair!'

Rapunzel had splendid long hair, as fine as spun gold, and when she heard the voice of the witch she undid her plaits, tied them to the window catch at the top, and then the rest of them fell down, twenty ells long, and the witch climbed up by them.

Now after a few years it so happened that the king's son was riding through the forest, and came past the tower. He heard singing so sweet that he stopped and listened. It was Rapunzel passing the time in her loneliness by listening to the sound of her voice. The king's son would have liked to climb up to her, and looked for the door to the tower, but there was none to be seen. He rode home, but her singing had touched his heart so, that very day he went out into the wood to listen to it. Once when he was standing behind a tree he saw the witch come and heard her say:

'Rapunzel, Rapunzel,
Let down your hair!'

Rapunzel let down her plaits, and the witch climbed up. 'If that is the ladder that leads up the tower I'll try my luck too,' thought he. And the next day, when it began to grow dark, he went to the tower and called:

'Rapunzel, Rapunzel,
Let down your hair!'

At once the plaits came down, and the king's son went up.

At first Rapunzel was very frightened when a man came into her room, for she had never seen a man before, but the king's son began to talk to her in quite a friendly way, and told her his heart had been so moved by her singing that it would give him no peace until he had seen her. Then Rapunzel lost her fear, and when he asked her if she would take him for her husband, and she saw that he was young and handsome, she thought: 'He will love me more than the old Mistress Gothel' (for that was the name of the witch), and said she would, and put her hand in his hand. She said: 'I will be glad to go with you, but I do not know how to get down. Every time you come bring a strand of silk, and I will twist a ladder out of it, and when it is ready I will climb down it and you shall take me away on your horse.'

They agreed then that he should come every evening, for the witch came by day. The old woman noticed nothing of all this, until one day Rapunzel happened to say to her: 'Tell me, Mistress Gothel, how is it that you are much heavier to pull up than the young king's son, who is up the tower in a moment?' 'Oh, you wretched girl!' cried the witch, 'what is this I hear? I thought I had kept you apart from all the world, and yet you have deceived me!' In her rage she seized Rapunzel's plaits, wound them a few times round her left hand, and—snip, snap!—she cut them off, and the beautiful hair lay on the ground. And she was so heartless that she drove Rapunzel away into a wilderness, where she had to live in great misery and wretchedness.

Now the same day that she sent Rapunzel away the witch tied the plait that she had cut off to the window-catch, and in the evening when the king's son came and called:

> 'Rapunzel, Rapunzel,
> Let down your hair!'

the witch let the hair down. The king's son climbed up, but at the top he found, not his dear Rapunzel, but the witch, who looked at him with angry, spiteful eyes. 'Aha,' she cried scornfully, 'you have come to fetch your dear wife, but that pretty bird no longer sits singing in this nest.

The cat has caught her, and now it will scratch your eyes out too. You have lost Rapunzel; you will never see her again.' The king's son was beside himself with grief; and in his despair he jumped down from the tower. He escaped with his life, but the thorns in which he landed scratched out his eyes.

Then he wandered blindly about the wood, eating only roots and berries, and did nothing but cry and sorrow over the loss of his dear wife. So for some years he wandered miserably about until at length he came to the wilderness, where Rapunzel lived with her little twins, a boy and a girl, in wretchedness. He heard a voice that he thought he knew, he went towards it, and when he reached the spot Rapunzel recognized him and fell on his neck and cried. But two of her tears fell on his eyes, so that they became clear, and he could see again as well as before. He took her to his kingdom, where he was received with joy, and there they lived happy and contented.

# The Iron Stove

IN the days when spells still worked, there was a witch who put a spell on a prince, binding him to sit in an iron stove in the middle of a forest. He spent many years there, and no one could set him free. One day there came into the forest a king's daughter who had lost herself and could not find her way back to her father's kingdom. For nine days she had wandered about, and now she found herself at last in front of the iron stove. A voice came from it, asking: 'Whence come you, and whither are you bound?'

She answered: 'I have lost my way to my father's kingdom and can't get home.' Then answered the voice out of the stove: 'I will help you home, and quickly too, if only you will undertake to do as I say. I am a greater prince than you are a princess, and I wish to marry you.' She was frightened, and thought to herself: 'Oh lord, what should

I do with an iron stove for a husband?' But because she wanted to go home to her father she promised to do as he told her. He said: 'You are to come back, bringing a knife with you, and scrape a hole in the iron.' Then he entrusted her to a companion who walked along beside her without speaking. But in two hours he had guided her home. Now there was great joy in the castle when the princess had come home, and the old king fell on her neck and kissed her. But she was much troubled and said: 'Dear father, what things have happened to me! I should never have got home out of that great wild wood if I had not happened on an iron stove, to which I had to promise to go back, set it free, and marry it.'

The old king was so frightened at that he nearly fell down in a faint, for he had only this one daughter. So they agreed to send the miller's daughter, who was beautiful, in her place. They took her out to the forest, gave her a knife, and told her to scrape the stove. She scraped away at it for four-and-twenty hours, but could not get the smallest bit of it off. As dawn was breaking there came a shout from inside the stove: 'I think it is light outside.' She answered: 'I think so too. It seems to me I can hear my father's mill working.' 'Then you are a miller's daughter; go away and send the princess back.' So she went and told the old king that the man in the wood did not want her, but the princess.

The old king was frightened, and his daughter wept. But they had a swineherd's daughter, who was even more beautiful than the miller's daughter, and they offered her a piece of gold if she would go to the iron stove instead of the king's daughter. So she was led out and scraped away for four-and-twenty hours. But neither could she get any of the iron off. As dawn was breaking there was a shout from the stove: 'I think it is light outside.' She answered: 'I think so too. It seems to me I can hear my father blowing his horn.'

'Then you are a swineherd's daughter; go straight away and send the princess back here; and tell her it shall go with her as I promised her, and if she does not come the whole kingdom will perish and fall to pieces so that not one stone is left on another.'

When the princess heard that she began to weep. But there was nothing for it but to abide by her promise. Then she said good-bye to her father, put a knife in her pocket, and went out to the iron stove in the forest. When she reached it she began to scrape and the iron gave way, so that by the time she had been at it for two hours she had made a little hole. She looked in, and saw such a handsome young man, all shimmering with gold and jewels, that her soul longed for him. So she went on scraping away until she had made the hole big enough for him to get out. Then he said: 'You are mine and I am yours; you are my betrothed come to set me free.'

He would have taken her with him into his own kingdom, but she excused herself, saying that she must go and see her father once more, which the prince allowed her to do; but she was only to speak three words to her father and then come back to him. She went home then, but she spoke more than three words. Then immediately the iron stove vanished and was taken far away across mountains of glass and sharp swords. But the king's son was free, and not shut up in it any more.

Then she took leave of her father and took some money with her, but not much, and went back to the forest to look for the iron stove; but she could not find it. Nine days she sought for it, until her hunger became so great that she did not know what to do, for she had nothing left to eat. When the evening came on she sat down in a little tree and thought she would spend the night there, because she was afraid of wild beasts.

When midnight came she saw a little light a long way off and thought: 'Now someone has come to take me away.' She climbed down from the tree and walked towards the light, praying as she went. She came to a little old cottage, all overgrown with grass, and a small pile of wood in front of it. 'Where have I got to now?' she thought, and looked in at the window. What should she see but a table spread with wine in silver cups and roast joints on silver plates, but no living thing except a little toad and a fat toad. She took heart and knocked at the door.

The fattest toad shouted:

> 'Little green girl,
> Hop-a-leg,
> Hop-a-leg's pup,
> Hop down, hop up,
> Go quick and see who's without.'

Then the little toad came to the door and opened it. When she came in they both made her welcome and asked her to sit down. 'Whence come you?' they asked, 'and whither are you going?' Then she told everything as it had befallen her, and how, because she had broken her word not to say more than three words to her father, the stove had gone away, together with the prince. Now she was off to look for it, over hill and dale, however long it might take her. Then the fattest toad said:

> 'Little green girl,
> Hop-a-leg,
> Hop-a-leg's pup,
> Hop down, hop up,
> And bring me the green box.'

The little toad went and brought the box. Then they gave her food and drink, and showed her to a nicely made bed, with sheets of silk and satin, and she lay down on it and slept after saying her prayers. When it was morning she got up, and the old toad took three needles out of the big box and gave them to her to take away. She would need them, for she would have to cross a glass mountain and three sharp-edged swords and a great lake. If she accomplished that journey she would find the prince again. The toad gave her three gifts: the three big needles, a plough wheel, and three nuts, and said she was to take care of them.

Then the princess set off, and when she came to the mountain of glass that was so smooth and slippery she drove in the needles behind and in front of her feet, and so she got over the mountain; she hid the needles in a place which she took care to remember exactly.

After that she came to the three sharp swords, but she got on to her plough wheel and rolled over them. At last she came to a large lake, and when she had crossed it, to a great castle. She went in and asked for work, saying that she was a poor maid looking for a job; but she knew that somewhere in the castle was the prince whom she had freed from the iron stove in the forest. So she was engaged as a kitchen-maid at a very low wage.

Now the king's son had with him another woman whom he wished to marry, for he had given the princess up for dead long ago. In the evening, when she had washed up and finished her work, the princess felt in her pocket and found the three nuts which the old toad had given her. She cracked one with her teeth, and was just going to eat the kernel when she saw that it contained a splendid royal robe. But when the prince's new sweetheart heard of this she came and offered to buy the robe, 'for' said she, 'it is no dress for a kitchen-maid.'

But no, the princess would not sell it; she might have the dress only if she would grant her one thing, and that was, to let her sleep one night in the bedroom of her betrothed. Because the dress was so beautiful and she had nothing like it herself, the prince's sweetheart agreed to this. In the evening she said to the prince: 'That silly girl wants to sleep in your room.' 'If you are content that she should, then so am I,' he said. But she gave him a glass of wine into which she had poured a sleeping draught. So both of them went into his room to sleep, and he slept so soundly the kitchen-maid could not waken him.

The kitchen-maid wept all night and cried: 'I saved you from the savage wood and the iron stove, I sought you across the glass mountain and the sharp swords and the great lake, and now that I have found you you will not listen to me.' The servants who were sitting outside the door of the room heard her crying all night long, and told their master in the morning. When she had washed up the next evening she cracked the second nut with her teeth, and there was an even finer dress inside it. When the prince's sweetheart saw it she wanted to buy it too. But the girl did not want money for it, asking as before to sleep in the prince's bedroom. His sweetheart gave him a sleeping draught so strong that he slept and heard nothing. But the kitchen-maid wept all night and cried: 'I saved you from the forest and the iron stove, and sought you across the glass mountain and the three sharp swords and the great lake, and yet you will not hear me.' The servants sitting outside the door heard her weeping all night long, and in the morning they told their master. On the third evening when she had finished washing up she cracked the third nut with her teeth, and found inside it the most beautiful dress, that shone like pure gold. As soon as the prince's sweetheart saw it she wanted to buy it, but the kitchen-maid would only part with it if she were allowed to sleep in the prince's bedroom. But this time the prince was wary and poured the sleeping draught away. As she began to weep and cry: 'Oh my darling, I saved you from the cruel savage forest and the iron stove,' he jumped up and cried: 'You're the true one at last. You are mine and I am yours.'

So that very night they got straight into a carriage, taking away with them his false sweetheart's clothes so that she could not get out of bed. When they came to the great lake they took ship across it, and when they came to the three sharp swords they rolled over them on the plough wheel, and when they came to the mountain of glass they climbed it by means of the three needles. So at last they got back to the little old cottage; but when they entered it it became a great castle: the toads had all been released from a spell and become princes and princesses, and were full of joy.

There the wedding feast was held, and they stayed in the castle, which was much larger than her father's castle. But because her old father complained of having to live all alone they set off and brought him back to live with them, and they had two kingdoms, and lived a happy married life.

A mouse is come
My story is done.

# Jorinda and Joringel

THERE was once an old castle, that stood in the middle
of a deep and gloomy wood, and in the castle lived an
old woman who was a witch of great power. All the day
long she flew about in the form of an owl, or crept about the
country like a cat; but at night she always became an old
woman again. She could lure birds and other game to her,
and these she cooked and ate. When any young man came
within a hundred paces of her castle, he became quite fixed,
and could not move a step till she came and set him free;

but when any pretty maiden came within that space she was changed into a bird, and the witch put her into a cage, and hung her up in a chamber in the castle. There were seven thousand of these cages hanging in the castle, and all with beautiful birds in them.

Now there was once a maiden whose name was Jorinda. She was prettier than all the pretty girls that ever were seen before, and a shepherd lad, whose name was Joringel, was very fond of her, and they were soon to be married. One day they went to walk in the wood, that they might be alone; and Joringel said: 'We must take care that we don't go too near to the witch's castle.' It was a beautiful evening; the last rays of the setting sun shone bright through the long trunks of the trees upon the green underwood beneath, and the turtle-doves sang from the tall birches.

Jorinda sat down and began to cry in the sunshine, Joringel sat crying by her side; and both felt sad, they knew not why; but it seemed to them as if they were to die. They had wandered a long way; and when they looked to see which way they should go home, they found themselves at a loss to know what path to take.

The sun was setting fast, and already half of its disk had sunk behind the hill; Joringel looked behind him, and saw through the bushes that they had, without knowing it, sat down close under the old walls of the castle. Then he was horror-stricken and turned pale. Jorinda was just singing:

> 'The ring-dove sang from the willow spray,
>     Well-a-day! Well-a-day!
>   He mourned for the fate of his darling mate,
>     Well-a-day! We-jug, jug, jug.'

Joringel turned, and beheld his Jorinda changed into a nightingale; so that her song ended with a mournful 'jug,

jug.' An owl with fiery eyes flew three times round them, and three times screamed:

'Tu whu! Tu whu! Tu whu!'

Joringel could not move; he stood fixed as a stone, and could neither weep, nor speak, nor stir a hand or foot. And now the sun went quite down; the gloomy night came; the owl flew into a bush, and a moment after an old woman came forth, yellow and skinny, with staring eyes, and a nose and chin that almost met one another.

She mumbled something to herself, seized the nightingale, and went away with it in her hand. Poor Joringel saw the nightingale was gone, but what could he do? He could not speak, he could not move from the spot where he stood. At last the old woman came back and said in a hoarse voice:

'Greeting, Zachiel!
When the moon shines in the cage,
Open it quickly!'

On a sudden Joringel found himself free. Then he fell on his knees before the old woman, and prayed her to give him back his dear Jorinda: but she laughed at him, and said he should never see her again; then she went her way.

He shouted, he wept, he sorrowed, but all in vain. 'Alas!' he said, 'what will become of me?' He could not go back to his own home, so he went to a strange village, and employed himself in keeping sheep. Many a time did he walk round and round as near to the hated castle as he dared go.

At last he dreamt one night that he found a beautiful blood-red flower, and that in the middle of it lay a costly pearl; and he dreamt that he plucked the flower, and went with it in his hand into the castle, and that everything he touched with it was disenchanted, and that there he found his Jorinda again.

In the morning when he awoke, he began to search over

hill and dale for this pretty flower, and eight long days he sought for it in vain; but on the ninth day, early in the morning, he found the beautiful blood-red flower; and in the middle of it was a large dew-drop, as big as the finest pearl. Then he plucked the flower, and set out and travelled day and night, till he came again to the castle.

He walked nearer than a hundred paces to the castle, and yet he did not become fixed as before, but found that he could go quite close up to the door. Joringel was very glad indeed to see this. Then he touched the door with the flower, and it sprang open, so that he went in through the court, and listened when he heard so many birds singing. At last he came to the chamber where the witch sat, with the seven thousand birds singing in seven thousand cages. When she saw Joringel she was very angry, and screamed with rage; but she could not come within two yards of him, for the flower he held in his hand was his safeguard. He took no notice of her but looked around at the birds; but alas! there were many, many nightingales, and how then should he find out which was his Joringa? While he was thinking what to do, he saw the witch had taken down one of the cages, and was making the best of her way through the door. He dashed after her, touched the cage and the witch with his flower. Now the witch could work no more spells, and his Jorinda stood before him and threw her arms round his neck, looking as beautiful as ever.

Then he touched all the other birds with the flower, so that they all took their old forms again; and he took Jorinda home, and they lived happily together many years.

# Hansel and Grethel

THERE was once a poor man, who was a woodman, and went every day to cut wood in a forest. One day as he went along, he heard a cry like a little child's; so he followed the sound, till at last he looked up a high tree, and on one of the branches sat a very little child. Now its mother had fallen asleep, and a vulture had taken it out of her lap and flown away with it, and left it on the tree. Then the woodcutter climbed up, took the little child down, and found it was a pretty little girl; and he said to himself: 'I will take this poor child home, and bring her up with my own son Hansel.' So he brought her to his cottage, and both grew up together: he called the little girl Grethel, and the two children were so very fond of each other that they were never happy but when they were together.

But the woodcutter became very poor, and had nothing in the world he could call his own; and indeed he had scarcely bread enough for his wife and the two children to eat. At last the time came when even that was all gone, and he knew not where to seek for help in his need. Then at night, as he lay on his bed, and turned himself here and there, restless and full of care, his wife said to him: 'Husband, listen to me, and take the two children out early to-morrow morning; give each of them a piece of bread, and then lead them into the midst of the wood, where it is thickest, make a fire for them, and go away and leave them alone to shift for themselves, for we can no longer keep them here.' 'No, wife,' said the husband, 'I cannot find it in my heart to leave the children to the wild beasts of the forest; they would soon tear them to pieces.' 'Well, if you will not do as I say,' answered the wife, 'we must all starve together.' And she would not let him have any peace until he came into her hard-hearted plan.

Meantime the poor children too were lying awake restless, and weak from hunger, so that they heard all that Hansel's mother said to her husband. 'Now,' thought Grethel to herself, 'it is all up with us'; and she began to weep. But Hansel crept to her bedside, and said: 'Do not be afraid, Grethel, I will find out some help for us.' Then he got up, put on his jacket, and opened the door and went out.

The moon shone bright upon the little court before the cottage, and the white pebbles glittered like daisies on the green meadows. So he stooped down, and put as many as he could into his pocket, and then went back to the house. 'Now, Grethel,' said he, 'rest in peace!' and he went to bed and fell fast asleep.

Early in the morning, before the sun had risen, the woodman's wife came and woke them. 'Get up, children,' said she, 'we are going into the wood, there is a piece of bread for each of you, but take care of it, and keep some for the afternoon.' Grethel took the bread, and carried it in her apron, because Hansel had his pocket full of stones; and they made their way into the wood.

After they had walked on for a time, Hansel stood still and looked towards home, and after a time he turned again, and so on several times. Then his father said: 'Hansel, why do you keep turning and lagging about so? Move on a little faster.' 'Ah, father,' answered Hansel, 'I am stopping to look at my white cat that sits on the roof, and wants to say good-bye to me.' 'You little fool!' said his mother, 'that is not your cat; it is the morning sun shining on the chimney-top.' Now Hansel had not been looking at the cat, but had all the while been lingering behind, to drop from his pocket one white pebble after another along the road.

When they came into the midst of the wood the woodman said: 'Run about, children, and pick up some wood, and I will make a fire to keep us all warm.' So they piled up a little heap of brushwood and set it on fire; and as the flames burnt brighter, the mother said: 'Now sit yourselves by the fire, and go to sleep, while we go and cut wood in the forest; be sure you wait till we come again and fetch you,' Hansel and Grethel sat by the fireside till the afternoon, and then each of them ate their piece of bread. They fancied the woodman was still in the wood, because they thought they heard the blows of his axe; but it was a bough, which he had cunningly hung upon a tree, in such a way that the wind blew it backwards and forwards against the other boughs; and so it sounded as the axe does in cutting.

Thus they waited till evening: but the woodman and his wife kept away, and no one came to fetch them.

When it was quite dark, Grethel began to cry; but then Hansel said: 'Wait till the moon rises.' And when the moon rose he took her by the hand, and there lay the pebbles along the ground, glittering like new pieces of money, and marking out the way. Towards morning they came again to the woodman's house, and he was glad in his heart when he saw the children again, for he had grieved at leaving them alone. His wife also seemed to be glad; but in her heart she was angry at it.

Not long afterwards there was again no bread in the house, and Hansel and Grethel heard the wife say to her husband: 'The children found their way back once, and I took it in good part; but now there is only half a loaf of bread left for them in the house; to-morrow you must take them deeper into the wood, that they may not find their way out, or we shall all be starved.' It grieved the husband in his heart to do as his selfish wife wished, and he thought it would be better to share their last morsel with the children; but as he had done as she had said once, he did not dare now to say no. When the children heard all their plan, Hansel got up, and wanted to pick up pebbles as before; but when he came to the door, he found his mother had locked it. Still he comforted Grethel, and said: 'Sleep in peace, dear Grethel! God is very kind, and will help us.'

Early in the morning, a piece of bread was given to each of them, but still smaller than the one they had before. Upon the road Hansel crumbled his in his pocket and often stood still, and threw a crumb upon the ground. 'Why do you lag so behind, Hansel?' said the woodman; 'go your way as before.' 'I am looking at my little dove that is sitting upon the roof, and wants to say good-bye to me.'

'You silly boy!' said the wife, 'that is not your little dove; it is the morning sun that shines on the chimney-top.' But Hansel still went on crumbling his bread and throwing it on the ground. And thus they went on still further into the wood, where they had never been before in all their life.

There they were again told to sit down by a large fire, and go to sleep; and the woodman and his wife said they would come in the evening and fetch them away. In the afternoon Hansel shared Grethel's bread, because he had strewed all his upon the road; but the day passed away, and evening passed away too, and no one came to the poor children. Still Hansel comforted Grethel, and said: 'Wait till the moon rises; and then I shall be able to see the crumbs of bread which I have strewed, and they will show us the way home.'

The moon rose; but when Hansel looked for the crumbs they were gone, for hundreds of little birds in the wood had found them and picked them up. Hansel, however, set out to try and find his way home; but they soon lost themselves in the wilderness, and went on through the night and all the next day, till at last they lay down and fell asleep for weariness. Another day they went on as before, but still did not come to the end of the wood; and they were as hungry as could be, for they had had nothing to eat.

In the afternoon of the third day they came to a strange little hut, made of bread, with a roof of cake, and windows of barley-sugar. 'Now we will sit down and eat till we have had enough,' said Hansel; 'I will eat off the roof for my share; do you eat the windows, Grethel, they will be nice and sweet for you.' Whilst Grethel, however, was picking at the barley-sugar, a pretty voice called softly from within:

'Tip, tap! who goes there?'

But the children answered:

'The wind, the wind,
That blows through the air!'

and went on eating. Now Grethel had broken out a round pane of the window for herself, and Hansel had torn off a large piece of cake from the roof, when the door opened, and a little old fairy came gliding out. At this Hansel and Grethel were so frightened, that they let fall what they had in their hands. But the old lady nodded to them, and said: 'Dear children, where have you been wandering about? Come in with me; you shall have something good.'

So she took them both by the hand, and led them into her little hut, and brought out plenty to eat—milk and pancakes, with sugar, apples, and nuts; and then two beautiful little beds were got ready, and Grethel and Hansel laid themselves down, and thought they were in heaven. But the fairy was a spiteful one, and made her pretty sweetmeat house to entrap little children. Early in the morning, before they were awake, she went to their little beds; and though she saw the two sleeping and looking so sweet, she had no pity on them, but was glad they were in her power. Then she took up Hansel, and fastened him in a coop by himself, and when he awoke he found himself behind a grating, shut up safely, as chickens are; but she shook Grethel, and called out: 'Get up, you lazy little thing, and fetch some water; and go into the kitchen, and cook something good to eat; your brother is shut up yonder. I shall first fatten him, and when he is fat, I think I shall eat him.'

When the fairy was gone poor Grethel bided her time, and got up, and ran to Hansel, and told him what she had heard, and said: 'We must run away quickly, for the old woman is a bad fairy, and will kill us.' But Hansel said: 'You must first steal away her fairy wand, that we may save ourselves if she should follow; and bring the pipe too that hangs up in her room.' Then the little maiden ran back, and fetched the magic wand and the pipe, and away they went together; so when the old fairy came back and could see no one at home, she sprang in a great rage to the window, and looked out into the wide world (which she could do far and near), and a long way off she spied Grethel, running away with her dear Hansel. 'You are already a great way off,' said she; 'but you will still fall into my hands.'

Then she put on her boots, which walked several miles at a step, and scarcely made two steps with them before she overtook the children; but Grethel saw that the fairy was coming after them, and, by the help of the wand, turned her friend Hansel into a lake of water, and herself into a swan, which swam about in the middle of it. So the fairy sat herself down on the shore, and took a great deal of trouble to decoy the swan, and threw crumbs of bread to it; but it would not come near her, and she was forced to go home in the evening, without taking her revenge. Then Grethel changed herself and Hansel back into their own forms once more, and they went journeying on the whole night, until the dawn of day, and then the maiden turned herself into a beautiful rose, that grew in the midst of a quickset hedge; and Hansel sat by the side.

The fairy soon came striding along. 'Good piper,' said she, 'may I pluck yon beautiful rose for myself?' 'Oh yes,' answered he. 'And then,' thought he to himself, 'I will play you a tune meantime.' So when she had crept into the hedge in a great hurry to gather the flower—for she well knew what it was—he pulled out the pipe slyly, and began to play. Now the pipe was a fairy pipe, and, whether

they liked it or not, whoever heard it was obliged to dance.
So the old fairy was forced to dance a merry jig, on and on
without any rest, and without being able to reach the rose.
And as he did not cease playing a moment, the thorns at
length tore the clothes from off her body, and pricked her
sorely, and there she stuck quite fast.

Then Grethel set herself free once more, and on they
went; but she grew very tired, and Hansel said: 'Now I
will hasten home for help.' And Grethel said: 'I will stay
here in the meantime, and wait for you.' Then Hansel
went away, and Grethel was to wait for him.

But when Grethel had stayed in the field a long time, and
found he did not come back, she became quite sorrowful,
and turned herself into a little daisy, and thought to herself:
'Someone will come and tread me underfoot, and so my
sorrows will end.' But it so happened that, as a shepherd
was keeping watch in the field, he saw the daisy; and
thinking it very pretty, he took it home, placed it in a box
in his room, and said: 'I have never found so pretty a daisy
before.' From that time everything throve wonderfully at
the shepherd's house. When he got up in the morning, all
the household work was ready done; the room was swept
and cleaned, the fire made, and the water fetched, and in
the afternoon, when he came home, the table-cloth was laid,
and a good dinner ready set for him. He could not make
out how all this happened, for he saw no one in his house;
and although it pleased him well enough, he was at length
troubled to think how it could be, and went to a cunning
woman who lived hard by, and asked her what he should do.
She said: 'There must be witchcraft in it; look out to-
morrow morning early, and see if anything stirs about in the
room: if it does, throw a white cloth at once over it, and
then the witchcraft will be stopped.' The shepherd did as

she said, and the next morning saw the box open, and the daisy come out: then he sprang up quickly, and threw a white cloth over it: in an instant the spell was broken and Grethel stood before him, for it was she who had taken care of his house for him; and she was so beautiful, that he asked her if she would marry him. She said 'No,' because she wished to be faithful to her dear Hansel; but she agreed to stay, and keep house for him till Hansel came back.

Time passed on, and Hansel came back at last, for the spiteful fairy had led him astray, and he had not been able for a long time to find his way, either home or back to Grethel. Then he and Grethel set out to go home; but after travelling a long way, Grethel became tired, and she and Hansel laid themselves down to sleep in a fine old hollow tree that grew in a meadow by the side of the wood. But as they slept the fairy—who had got out of the bush at last—came by; and finding her wand was glad to lay hold of it, and at once turned poor Hansel into a fawn while he was asleep.

Soon after Grethel awoke, and found what had happened; and she wept bitterly over the poor creature; and the tears too rolled down his eyes, and he laid himself down beside her. Then she said: 'Rest in peace, dear fawn; I will never, never leave thee.' She took off her golden necklace and put it round his neck, and plucked some rushes, and plaited them into a soft string to fasten to it, and led the poor little thing by her side when she went to walk in the wood; and when they were tired they came back, and lay down to sleep by the side of the hollow tree, where they lodged at night: but nobody came near them except the little dwarfs that lived in the wood, and these watched over them while they were asleep.

At last one day they came to a little cottage, and Grethel, having looked in and seen that it was quite empty, thought to herself: 'We can stay and live here.' Then she went and gathered leaves and moss to make a soft bed for the fawn; and every morning she went out and plucked nuts, roots, and berries for herself, and sweet shrubs and tender grass for her friend; and it ate out of her hand, and was pleased, and played and frisked about her. In the evening, when Grethel was tired, and had said her prayers, she laid her head upon the fawn for her pillow, and slept; and if poor Hansel could but have his right form again, she thought they should lead a very happy life.

They lived thus a long while in the wood by themselves, till it chanced that the king of that country came to hold a great hunt there. And when the fawn heard all around the echoing of the horns, and the baying of the dogs, and the merry shouts of the huntsmen, he wished very much to go and see what was going on. 'Ah, sister! sister!' said he, 'let me go out into the wood, I can stay no longer.' And he begged so long, that she at last agreed to let him go. 'But,' said she, 'be sure to come to me in the evening; I shall shut up the door, to keep out those wild huntsmen; and if you tap at it and say: "Sister, let me in!" I shall know you; but if you don't speak, I shall keep the door fast.' Then away sprang the fawn, and frisked and bounded along in the open air. The king and his huntsman saw the beautiful creature, and followed, but could not overtake him; for when they thought they were sure of their prize, he sprang over the bushes, and was out of sight at once.

As it grew dark he came running home to the hut and tapped, and said: 'Sister, sister, let me in!' Then she opened the little door, and in he jumped, and slept soundly all night on his soft bed.

Next morning the hunt began again, and when he heard the huntsmen's horns, he said: 'Sister, open the

door for me, I must go again.' Then she let him out, and
said: 'Come back in the evening, and remember what you
are to say.' When the king and the huntsmen saw the
fawn with the golden collar again, they gave him chase;
but he was too quick for them. The chase lasted the
whole day; but at last the huntsmen nearly surrounded
him, and one of them wounded him in the foot, so that
he became sadly lame, and could hardly crawl home. The
man who had wounded him followed close behind, and hid
himself, and heard the little fawn say: 'Sister, sister, let
me in!' upon which the door opened, and soon shut again.
The huntsman marked all well, and went to the king and
told him what he had seen and heard; then the king said:
'To-morrow we will have another chase.'

Grethel was very much frightened when she saw that
her dear little fawn was wounded; but she washed the
blood away, and put some healing herbs on it, and said:
'Now go to bed, dear fawn, and you will soon be well
again.' The wound was so slight, that in the morning
there was nothing to be seen of it; and when the horn
blew, the little thing said: 'I can't stay here, I must go
and look on; I will take care that none of them shall catch
me.' But Grethel said: 'I am sure they will kill you this
time: I will not let you go.' 'I shall die of grief,' said he,
'if you keep me here; when I hear the horns, I feel as
if I could fly.' Then Grethel was forced to let him go:
so she opened the door with a heavy heart, and he bounded
out gaily into the wood.

When the king saw him, he said to the huntsmen: 'Now
chase him all day long, till you catch him; but let none of
you do him any harm.' The sun set, however, without
their being able to overtake him, and the king called away
the huntsmen, and said to the one who had watched: 'Now

come and show me the little hut.' So they went to the door and tapped, and said: 'Sister, sister, let me in!' Then the door opened, and the king went in, and there stood a maiden more lovely than any he had ever seen. Grethel was frightened to see that it was not her fawn but the king with a golden crown that was come into her hut: however, he spoke kindly to her, and took her hand, and said: 'Will you come with me to my castle, and be my wife?' 'Yes,' said the maiden, 'I will go to your castle, but I cannot be your wife, and my fawn must go with me, I cannot part with that.' 'Well,' said the king, 'he shall come and live with you all your life, and want for nothing.' Just then in sprang the little fawn; and his sister tied the string to his neck, and they left the hut in the wood together.

Then the king took Grethel to his palace, and on the way she told him all her story: and then he sent for the fairy, and made her change the fawn into Hansel again; and he and Grethel loved one another, and were married, and lived happily together all their days in the good king's palace.

# The Boy who set out to Learn What Fear Was

A FATHER had two sons, of whom one was clever and
sensible and acquitted himself well in everything, but
the younger one was so stupid that he could not understand

or learn anything. Whenever people saw him, they said: 'His father will have his hands full with him.' When anything was to be done, the eldest son was able to deal with it himself; but if his father told him to go and fetch something in the evening or at night, and the way led through the churchyard or some such creepy place, he would answer: 'Oh no, father, I won't go, it makes my flesh creep!' for he was afraid. Or when they were sitting round the fire in the evenings, telling stories that made their hair stand on end, often the company would say: 'Oh, it makes my flesh creep!' The younger son would be sitting in the corner listening, and could not understand what they meant. 'They keep on saying it makes their flesh creep, but mine doesn't. It must be one of those arts I do not understand.'

Now one day his father chanced to say to him: 'Listen, you there in the corner, you are growing big and strong; you must learn a trade to earn your living by. Look at the trouble your brother takes, while you are not worth your keep.' 'Well, father,' he answered, 'I should be glad to learn anything. I would learn flesh-creeping, if it came to that. I don't know anything about that.' The elder son laughed when he heard that, thinking to himself: 'Lord, what a fool my brother is! He'll never make anything of his life. The twig that will become a crook, must learn to bend early in life.' His father sighed and replied: 'We'll teach you to feel your flesh creep, but you won't earn your living by it.'

Soon after that the sexton came to visit the family, and the old man told him his difficulties, and told him how his younger son was so unhandy at everything that he knew nothing and learnt nothing. 'Only think, when I asked him how he was going to earn his living, he said he wanted to learn to feel his flesh creep.' 'If that is all he wants,' answered the sexton, 'I can teach him that. Just send him to me and I'll soon lick him into shape.' His father was pleased with this, thinking: 'This will help the lad along.' So he was taken into the sexton's house, and his job was to ring the bells. A few days later the sexton woke him at midnight, telling him to get up, go to the church tower, and ring the bells. 'You will soon feel your flesh creep,' he thought, and he went out secretly before him, and when the lad had got up the tower, and went to take hold of the bell-rope, he saw a white figure standing on the stairs over against the trap-door of the bell-loft. 'Who's there?' he shouted, but the figure gave no answer, neither did it move or budge. 'Answer me,' the lad shouted, 'or else go away. You have no business here by night.' But the sexton did not stir, so as to make the lad think he was a ghost. For the second time the youngster shouted: 'What do you want with me? If you are an honest man, speak, or I will throw you downstairs.' The sexton thought: 'He doesn't really mean it,' and he made no sound but stood stock still. The lad challenged him for the third time, but without result. So he took a run at the ghost and kicked it downstairs, so that it fell ten steps and lay in a corner.

Then he rang his peal, went home, went to bed without saying anything, and fell asleep. The sexton's wife waited a long time for her husband but he did not come home. At last she grew anxious and woke the lad, asking him: 'Do you know where my husband is? He went to the church tower before you did.' 'No,' he replied. 'But there was someone standing on the trap-door by the stairs, and as he would neither answer me nor go away I thought he was up to no good and kicked him downstairs. Go to the church and see if that was he; I'm sorry if it was.' She hurried off and found her husband, lying in a corner, and groaning with a broken leg.

She carried him down and rushed off shouting to the boy's father. 'Your son,' she cried, 'has done us much harm. He has thrown my husband downstairs and broken his leg. Take the good-for-nothing out of my house.' The father was shocked; he came running and scolded his son. 'What kind of unholy tricks are these?' he said. 'The evil one must have put them into your head.' 'Father,' he said, 'listen to me. I am quite innocent. He came and stood there in the night like someone up to no good. I did not know who it was, and I warned him three times to speak or go away.' 'Ah,' said his father, 'I get nothing but trouble from you. Get out of my sight, I cannot bear you near me any longer.' 'Certainly I will, father, only wait until it is light, then I will go and learn to feel my flesh creep, so that I shall have a trade to earn my living by.' 'Learn what you like,' said his father. 'It's all one to me. Here are fifty thalers; now go out into the wide world and tell no one whose son you are or where you come from, for I am ashamed of you.' 'Yes, father, just as you say, if you ask no more of me I can easily remember that.'

When dawn came, he put his fifty thalers in his pocket, and walked off along the high road, muttering to himself: 'If only my flesh would creep, if only my flesh would creep!' Then he met a man who heard him talking to himself, and when they had gone a little further and come in sight of the gallows, the man said to him: 'Look now, that is the tree where seven men married the ropewalker's daughter, and now they are learning to fly. Sit down under it and wait for nightfall. Then your flesh will creep.' 'If that's all there is to it,' answered the youth, 'it's easy enough. If I learn as quickly as all that, you shall have my fifty thalers;

come and see me to-morrow morning.' So he went up to the gallows, sat down underneath it, and waited for night to fall. Because he was cold, he lit a fire; but about midnight the wind blew so cold that he could not get warm in spite of the fire. When the wind began to blow the hanged men against each other so that they swung to and fro, he thought: 'You are cold enough down here by the fire; how they must be freezing and shivering up there!' Because he was sorry for them, he set up the ladder, climbed up, and cut them down, one by one, and carried all seven to the fire. He stirred the fire and blew it up, and sat them all round it to warm themselves. But they sat there without moving and their clothes caught fire. 'Take care,' he said, 'or I will hang you all up again.' But the dead men did not listen, they kept silent and let their rags burn away. He grew angry, and said to them: 'If you will not help yourselves I cannot help you. I do not wish to get burnt along with you.' So he hung them all up again, one by one. Then he sat down again by his fire, and went to sleep until the morning, when the man came back to fetch his fifty thalers, and asked: 'Now, did your flesh creep?' 'No,' he answered, 'why should it? Those men up there never opened their mouths, and they were so stupid that they let the few rags they had on burn away.' The man, seeing that he would not get his fifty thalers that day, went away, saying: 'I never met any one like that before.'

The lad too went on his way, and again began to mutter to himself: 'Oh, if only my flesh would creep, if only my flesh would creep!' A carrier, who was walking behind him, heard that and asked: 'Who are you?' 'I do not know!' answered the lad. 'Where are you from?' asked the carrier. 'I do not know,' answered the lad. 'Who is your father?' 'I may not say!' 'What do you keep on muttering to yourself?' 'Oh!' answered the youth, 'I wish my flesh would creep, but no one will teach me how it is done.' 'Enough of that silly talk!' said the carrier. 'Come with me. I will find you a lodging.' The lad went along with him, and in the evening they came to an inn, where they were to spend the night. As he went into the parlour he said again out loud: 'If only my flesh would creep!' The landlord heard him and laughed. 'If that's what you're after, you've come to the right place.' 'Be silent,' said his wife. 'So many a clever young man has lost his life, it would be pity and a shame for his beautiful eyes if he were never to see the light of day again.' The lad said: 'I will learn, however hard it is, for that is why I set out from home.'

He would not leave the landlord in peace until he told him how not far from the inn there was a haunted castle, where anybody's flesh would creep if they would only spend three nights there. The king had promised the man who should dare to do it his daughter's hand, and she was the fairest maiden the sun ever shone on; in the castle there were great treasures guarded by evil spirits. If they could be released they would make a poor man rich enough. Many men had gone in, but so far no one had come out again. The next morning the lad went before the king and said: 'If I may, I would like to watch three nights in the haunted castle.' The king looked him up and down, and because he liked him he said: 'You may ask for three things, but they must be lifeless things, and you may take them into the castle with you.' He answered: 'Then I ask for a fire, a lathe, and a carving-bench with a knife.'

During daylight the king had all these things carried into the castle for him. As night was coming on, the lad went up to the castle, lit a bright fire in one of the rooms, set the carving-bench and the knife close to it, and sat down on the lathe-bench. 'Ah, if only my flesh would creep!' he said, 'but it will not happen here either.' About midnight he was going to poke his fire; as he was blowing it up, there came a screech from the corner: 'Miaow! We are cold!' 'You fools,' he said. 'What are you screeching for? If you are cold, come and sit by the fire and warm yourselves.' No sooner had he said that, than two black cats came leaping out, and sat down on either side of him, looking at him wildly out of their great fiery eyes. After a little while, when they had warmed themselves, they said: 'Now, my friend, shall we have a little game of cards?' 'Why not?' he answered. 'But first let me see your paws.' So they stretched out their paws. 'Oh,' said he, 'what long nails you have! Wait till I trim them for you.' With that he seized them by the scruff of their necks, lifted them on to the carving-bench, and screwed down their paws. 'Now that I have seen your fingers,' he said, 'I don't feel so inclined to play cards.' He killed them and threw them out into the moat.

When he had disposed of them and was about to sit down by his fire again, hosts of black dogs and cats on red-hot chains came at him from all sides, more and more of them, so that he could not get away from them. They howled horribly, trod on his fire and scattered it, and tried to put it out. For a moment he looked on quietly, but when he could stand no more he snatched up the carving-knife and shouted: 'Away with you, you rabble!' and went for them. Some of them ran away, some he killed and threw out of the window into the moat.

When he had finished he blew up the fire again from the embers and warmed himself by it. As he sat there his eyelids began to droop so that he longed for sleep. He looked in the corner and saw a great bed there. 'Just the thing for me,' he said, and got into it. As he was going to shut his eyes the bed began to move of itself, and travelled all round the castle. 'That's good,' he said, 'just what I wanted.' The bed rolled along as if six horses were harnessed to it, through the doors and up and down the stairs; suddenly it turned over with a crash, and lay on top of him like a mountain. But he threw off the mattresses and pillows, climbed out, and said: 'Someone else can sleep in the travelling bed.' He lay down again by his fire and slept until it was light. In the morning the king arrived, and, seeing him lying there on the floor, thought he was dead and that the ghosts had killed him. 'Woe is me for the fine young man,' said he. The lad heard him, sat up and said: 'It has not come to that yet!' The king was astonished but glad, and asked him how things had gone. 'Very well,' he replied. 'One night has passed and the other two will pass also.' Then he went to see the landlord, who gaped at him. 'Little did I think,' said he, 'to see you alive again; did your flesh creep?' 'No,' said he, 'it was all in vain. If only someone would teach me!'

The second night he went up to the old castle again, sat down by the fire, and began as usual to harp away on the old tune—'If only my flesh would creep.' On the stroke of midnight, there was a loud noise of something bumping about, softly at first, then louder and louder, then silence for a moment; then there was a yell and half a man came down the chimney and fell at his feet. 'Hallo,' he said, 'there should be another half to come. That's not enough by itself.' Then the noise began again, with knocking and howling, and the other half fell down too. 'Wait a bit,' said he, 'I'll blow up the fire for you.' When he had done that and looked round, the two halves had joined up to make a grey-haired man who was sitting in his seat. 'We didn't bargain for that,' said the lad. 'That's my bench.'

The man tried to push him away, but the lad would not have

it, shoved him roughly away, and sat down on his own seat again. Then more men came down the chimney, one after another, bringing two skulls and nine thigh-bones. These they set up and began to play skittles. The lad became interested and asked if he might play with them. 'Yes,' they said, 'if you have any money.' 'Plenty of money!' he said. 'But your balls are not properly round.' He took the skulls, put them on the lathe and turned them round. 'Now they'll roll,' he said. 'Now for some fun!' He played a game with them and lost some money to them, but when midnight struck everything vanished from his sight. He lay down and went quietly to sleep. In the morning the king came and asked for news. 'What happened this time?' he asked. 'I played a game of skittles,' was the answer, 'and lost a halfpenny or two.' 'Did not your flesh creep?' 'Why should it? I was enjoying myself! If only I knew what it meant!'

On the third night he sat down again on his bench, grumbling quite crossly: 'I wish my flesh would creep.' In the evening six tall men came in carrying a coffin. 'Aha,' he said, 'that must be my little cousin who died the other day.' He beckoned with his finger, calling: 'Come here, cousin.' They put the coffin down on the floor, and he went up to it and took off the lid. A dead man lay inside. He felt his face but it was as cold as ice. 'Wait,' said he, 'I'll warm you a little'; and he went to the fire, warmed his hand at it, and laid it on the dead man's face; but still he stayed cold. So he took him out of the coffin, and sat down at the fire with him in his lap, rubbing his arms to make the blood run round again. When that failed, he thought: 'If two people get into bed together, that warms them up,' so he put him into the bed, made up the coverlets, and lay down beside him. By and by the dead man began to get warm and to move. The young man said: 'Now look, cousin, haven't I warmed you up?' But the dead man began to shout: 'I will kill you!' 'What!' said he, 'is that all the thanks I get? Back you go into your coffin.' He picked him up, threw him back again, and shut the lid. Then the six men came back and carried him away again. 'My flesh won't creep,' he said. 'I'll never learn that here if I stay all my life!'

Then there came a man taller than all the others; he looked frightful; but he was old, with a long white beard. 'Now, you wretch,' he cried, 'I'll make your flesh creep. You are to die!' 'Not so fast,' answered the lad. 'If I am to die, I must have something to say to it.' 'I'll soon settle you,' said the monster.' 'Softly, softly, don't be so cock-sure. I'm as strong as you, and stronger.' 'We shall see,' said the old man. 'If you are stronger than I, I will let you go free. Let us put it to the proof.' He led him along dark corridors to a blacksmith's forge, took an axe, and struck one of the anvils into the ground at one blow. 'I can do better than that,' said the lad. He went to the other anvil; the old man stood beside him, watching what he would do, and his white beard was hanging down. The youth took up the axe, split the anvil at one blow, and jammed the old man's beard into it. 'Now I've got you,' he said. 'Now it is your turn to die!' Then he took an iron bar and beat the old man with it, until he whimpered and begged the lad to stop, for he would give him great riches. The lad pulled the axe out of the crack, releasing his beard. The old man led him back through the castle, and showed him a cellar where there were three chests full of gold. 'One of these,' he said, 'is for the poor, the second for the king, and the third is yours.' At that moment it struck twelve, and the spirit vanished, so that the lad was left in darkness.

'I shall yet find my way out,' he said.   He felt his way about and found the way into his room, where he went to sleep by his fire.   The king came to see him in the morning, and said: 'Have you learnt now what it is for your flesh to creep?'   'No,' he answered, 'why should I?   My dead cousin came here, and a man with a beard came and showed me a great deal of money.   But no one said anything about my flesh creeping.'   Then the king said: 'You have laid the ghost of the castle, and you shall marry my daughter.'   'That is all very well,' he answered, 'but I still do not know anything about my flesh creeping.'

Then the gold was brought up and the wedding feast was held, but the lad who had become a king, for all that he was so contented and loved his wife so much, kept on saying: 'If only my flesh would creep!'   At last she got tired of it.   Her chambermaid said to her: 'I will help him to learn all about that.'   Out she went to the stream that flowed through the garden and caught a pailful of gudgeon.   That night, when the young king was asleep, she told his wife to pull off the bed-clothes and empty the bucketful of cold water over him, gudgeon and all.   The little fishes flapped around him in the bed.   Then he awoke and shouted: 'Oh, how my flesh creeps, how it creeps, dear wife!   Yes, now I know what it means!'

# Donkey-Wort

A merry huntsman was once riding briskly along through a wood, now winding his horn and now singing a merry song. As he journeyed along, there came up a little old woman and said to him: 'Good day, good day, dear huntsman. You seem merry enough, but I am hungry and thirsty; do pray give me something to eat.' So he took pity on her and put his hand in his pocket and gave her what he had. Then he was about to go his way; but she took hold of him and said: 'Listen, master huntsman, to what I am going to tell you. I will reward you for your kindness. Go your way, and after a little time you will come to a tree, where you will see nine birds sitting with a cloak in their claws which they are tugging to and fro. Shoot into the midst of them, and one will fall down dead. The cloak will fall, too. Take it as a wishing-cloak, and when you

94

wear it you will find yourself at any place you may wish to be. Cut open the dead bird, take out its heart and swallow it, and you will find a piece of gold under your pillow every morning when you rise. It is the bird's heart that will bring you this good luck.'

The huntsman thanked her, and thought to himself: 'If all this happens it will be a fine thing for me.' When he had gone a hundred paces or so, he heard a screaming and chirping in the branches above him; so he looked up, and saw a flock of birds pulling a cloak with their bills and feet, screaming, fighting, and tugging at each other as if each wished to have it himself.

'Well,' said the huntsman, 'this is wonderful; this happens just as the old woman said.' Then he shot into the midst of them, so that their feathers flew all about. Off went the flock chattering away; but one fell down dead and the cloak with it. Then he did as the old woman told him, cut open the bird, took out its heart and swallowed it, and carried the cloak home with him.

The next morning when he awoke he lifted up his pillow, and there lay the piece of gold glittering underneath; the same thing happened next day, and indeed every day when he arose. He heaped up a great deal of gold, and at last thought to himself: 'Of what use is this gold to me whilst I am at home? I will go out into the world and look about me.'

Then he took leave of his friends and hung his horn and gun about his shoulders and went his way merrily as before.

Now it happened that his road led through a thick wood at the end of which was a large castle in a green meadow; and at one of the windows stood an old woman with a very beautiful maiden by her side, looking about them. The old woman was a witch, and she said to the maiden: 'Here comes a young man out of the wood with a wonderful prize; we must get it away from him, my dear child, for it is more fit for us than for him. He has a bird's heart that brings a piece of gold under his pillow each morning.' Then she told her how they would set about it, and what her part was to be; and finally she threatened her and said with a spiteful look: 'And if you disobey me, so much the worse for you!'

Meanwhile the huntsman came nearer, and as he looked at the girl he said to himself: 'I have been travelling so long that I should like to go into this castle and rest myself, for I have money enough to pay for everything I want.' But the real reason was that he wanted to see more of the beautiful girl. Then he went into the house, and was kindly welcomed; and it was not long before he was so much in love, that he thought of nothing else but looking in the witch-maiden's eyes, and doing everything that she wished. Then the old woman said: 'Now is the time to get the bird's heart.' So they made a magic drink, and when it was ready they poured it into a cup and the witch-maiden handed it to the huntsman, saying: 'Now, my dearest, drink to me.' So he took the cup and drank it, and brought up the bird's heart. Then the witch-girl stole it away and swallowed it herself and he never found any more gold under his pillow, for it lay now under hers, and the old woman took it away each morning; but he was so much in love that he never missed his prize.

'Well,' said the old witch, 'we have got the bird's heart, but not the wishing-cloak yet, and that we must also get.' 'Let us leave him that!' said the maiden. 'He has already lost all his wealth.' Then the witch was very angry and said: 'Such a cloak is a very rare and wonderful thing, and I must have it!' Then she beat her and said if she would not obey it would be the worse for her. So she did as the old woman told her, and sat herself at the window, and looked about the country, and seemed very sorrowful. Then the huntsman said: 'What makes you so sad?' 'Alas, my dear,' she said, 'yonder lies the granite rock, where all the precious diamonds grow, and I want so much to go there that, whenever I think of it, I cannot help being sorrowful, for who can reach it? Only the birds of the air—man cannot.' 'If that's all your grief,' said the huntsman, 'I'll take you there with all my heart.' So he drew her under his cloak, and the moment he wished to be on the granite mountain, they were both there.

The diamonds glittered so on all sides that they were delighted with the sight, and picked up the finest. But the old witch made deep drowsiness come upon him: and he said to the maiden: 'Let us sit down and rest ourselves a little, I am so tired that I cannot stand any longer.' So they sat down, and he laid his head in her lap and fell asleep; and whilst he was sleeping on, the false maiden took the cloak from his shoulders, hung it on her own, picked up the diamonds, and wished herself at her own home again.

When the poor huntsman awoke and found his lover had tricked him, and left him alone on the wild rock, he said: 'Alas! What roguery there is in the world!' And there he sat in great grief and fear upon the mountain, not knowing what in the world he should do.

Now this rock belonged to fierce giants who lived upon it, and as he saw three of them striding about, he thought to himself: 'I can only save myself by feigning to be asleep.' So he laid himself down, as if he were in a sound sleep. When the giants came up to him, the first kicked him with his boot and said: 'What worm is this that lies curled up here?' 'Tread on him and kill him!' said the second. 'It's not worth the trouble,' said the third; 'let him live:

he will go climbing higher up the mountain, and some cloud will come rolling up and carry him away.' Then they passed on. But the huntsman had heard all they said and as soon as they were gone he climbed to the top of the mountain: and when he had sat there a short time, a cloud came rolling around him and caught him up in a whirlwind, and bore him along for some time till it settled in a garden, where he fell quite gently to the ground among the greens and cabbages.

Then the huntsman got up and scratched his head and looked round him and said: 'I wish I had something to eat: if I have not I shall be worse off than before; for here I see neither apples nor pears nor any kind of fruits; nothing but vegetables.' At last he thought to himself: 'I can at least eat salad; it is not very tasty but it will refresh and strengthen me.' So he picked out a fine head of some plant that he took for a salad and ate of it; but scarcely had he swallowed two bites, when he felt himself quite changed, and saw with horror that he was turned into an ass. However, he still felt hungry, and the green herbs tasted very nice; so he ate on till he came to another plant, which looked very like the first; but it really was quite different, for he had scarcely tasted it when he felt another change come over him, and soon saw that he was lucky enough to have found his old shape.

Then he laid himself down and slept off a little of his weariness; and when he awoke next morning he broke off a head of each sort of salad, thinking to himself: 'This will help me to my fortune again, and enable me to punish some folks for their treachery.' So he set about trying to find the castle of his sweetheart, and, after wandering about for a few days, he luckily found it. Then he stained his face all over brown, so that even his mother would not have known him, and went into the castle and asked for a lodging. 'I am so tired,' said he, 'that I can go no further.' 'Countryman,' said the witch, 'who are you? And what is your business?' 'I am,' said he, 'a messenger sent by the king to find the finest salad that grows under the sun. I have been lucky enough to find it, and have brought it with me: but the heat of the sun is so scorching that it begins to wither, and I don't know that I can carry it any further.'

When the witch and the maiden heard of this beautiful salad, they longed to taste it, and said: 'Dear country-man, do let us have a taste!' 'To be sure,' said he, 'I have two heads of it with me, and I will give you one.' So he opened the bag and gave them the bad sort. Then the witch herself took it into the kitchen to be dressed; and when it was ready she could not wait till it was carried up, but took a few leaves immediately and put them in her mouth; but scarcely they were swallowed when she lost her own form, and ran braying down into the courtyard in the form of an ass.

Now the servant-girl came into the kitchen, and seeing the salad was ready was going to carry it up; but on the way she too felt a wish to taste it, as the old woman had done, and ate some leaves; so she also was turned into an ass, and ran after the other, letting the dish of salad fall to the ground.

The huntsman had been sitting all this time chatting with the fair maiden, and as nobody came with the salad, and she longed to taste it, she said: 'I don't know where that salad can be.' Then he thought something must have happened, and said: 'I will go into the kitchen and see.' And as he went he saw two asses in the courtyard running about, and the salad lying on the ground. 'All right,' said he, 'those two have had their share.' Then he picked up the rest of the leaves, laid them on the dish, and brought them to the maiden, saying: 'I bring you the dish myself, so that you need not wait any longer.' So she ate of it, and, like the others, ran off on to the courtyard braying away.

Then the huntsman washed his face and went into the courtyard, so that they might know him. 'Now you shall be paid for your roguery,' said he, and tied them all three to a rope, and took them along with him, till he came to a mill and knocked at the window. 'What's the matter?' said the miller. 'I have three tiresome beasts here,' said the other, 'that I do not wish to keep. If you will take them, give them food and stabling, and treat them as I tell you, I will pay you whatever you ask.' 'With all my heart,' said the miller, 'but how shall I treat them?' Then the huntsman said: 'Give the old one stripes three times a day and hay once: give the next (who was the maid-servant) stripes once a day and hay three times: and give the youngest (who was the pretty witch-maiden) hay three times a day and no stripes.' For he could not find it in his heart to have her beaten. After this he went back to the castle, where he found everything he wanted.

Some days after the miller came to him and told him the old ass was dead. 'The other two,' says he, 'are alive and eating; but they are so sorrowful that they cannot last long.' Then the huntsman had pity on them and told the miller to drive them back to him, and when they came he gave them some of the good salad to eat.

The moment they had eaten, they were both changed into their right forms, and the beautiful maiden fell on her knees before him and said: 'Forgive me all the wrong I have done you; my mother forced me to do it, and it was sorely against my will, for I have always loved you well. Your wishing-cloak is hanging in the cupboard. And as for the bird's heart, I will give you that too.' 'No,' he said, 'keep it. It will be just the same thing in the end, for I mean to make you my wife.'

So they were married and lived together very happily until they died.

# Old Sultan

A SHEPHERD had a faithful dog, called Sultan, who was grown very old, and had lost all his teeth. And one day when the shepherd and his wife were standing together before the house the shepherd said: 'I shall shoot old Sultan to-morrow morning, for he is of no use now.' But his wife said: 'Pray let the poor faithful creature live; he has served us well a great many years, and we ought to give him a livelihood for the rest of his days.' 'But what can we do with him?' said the shepherd, 'he has not a tooth in his head, and the thieves don't care for him at all; to be sure he has served us, but then he did it to earn his livelihood; to-morrow shall be his last day, depend upon it.'

Poor Sultan, who was lying close to them, heard all that the shepherd and his wife said to one another, and was very much frightened to think to-morrow would be his last day; so in the evening he went to his good friend the wolf, who lived in the wood, and told him all his sorrows, and how his master meant to kill him in the morning. 'Make yourself easy,' said the wolf, 'I will give you some good advice. Your master, you know, goes out every morning very early with his wife into the field; and they take their little child with them, and lay it down behind the hedge in the shade while they are at work. Now do you lie down close by the child, and pretend to be watching it, and I will come out of the wood and run away with it; you must run after me as fast as you can, and I will let it drop; then you may carry it back, and they will think you have saved their child, and will be so thankful to you that they will take care of you as long as you live.' The dog liked this plan very well; and accordingly so it was managed. The wolf ran with the child a little way; the shepherd and his wife screamed out; but Sultan soon overtook him, and carried the poor little thing back to his master and mistress. Then the shepherd patted him on the head, and said: 'Old Sultan has saved our child from the wolf, and therefore he shall live and be well taken care of, and have plenty to eat. Wife, go home, and give him a good dinner, and let him have my old cushion to sleep on as long as he lives.' So from this time forward Sultan had all that he could wish for.

Soon afterwards the wolf came and wished him joy, and said: 'Now, my good fellow, you must tell no tales, but turn your head the other way when I want to taste one of the old shepherd's fine fat sheep.' 'No,' said Sultan; 'I will be true to my master.' However, the wolf thought he was joking, and came one night to get a dainty morsel. But Sultan had told his master what the wolf meant to do; so he laid wait for him behind the barn door, and when the wolf was busy looking out for a good fat sheep, he had a stout cudgel laid about his back, that combed his locks for him finely.

Then the wolf was very angry, and called Sultan 'an old rogue,' and swore he would have his revenge. So the next morning the wolf sent the boar to challenge Sultan to come into the wood to fight the matter out. Now Sultan had nobody he could ask to be his second but the shepherd's old three-legged cat; so he took her with him, and as the poor thing limped along with some trouble, she stuck up her tail straight in the air.

The wolf and the wild boar were first on the ground; and when they espied their enemies coming, and saw the cat's long tail standing straight in the air, they thought she was carrying a sword for Sultan to fight with; and every time she limped, they thought she was picking up a stone to throw at them; so they said they should not like this way of fighting, and the boar lay down behind a bush, and the wolf jumped up into a tree. Sultan and the cat soon came up, and looked about and wondered that no one was there. The boar, however, had not quite hidden himself, for his ears stuck out of the bush, and when he shook one of them a little, the cat, seeing something move, and thinking it was a mouse, sprang upon it, and bit and scratched it, so that the boar jumped up and grunted, and ran away, roaring out: 'Look up in the tree, there sits the one who is to blame.' So they looked up, and espied the wolf sitting amongst the branches; and they called him a cowardly rascal, and would not suffer him to come down till he was heartily ashamed of himself, and had promised to be good friends again with old Sultan.

# The Fox and the Horse

A FARMER had a horse that had been an excellent
faithful servant to him: but he was now grown too old to
work; so the farmer would give him nothing more to eat, and
said: 'I want you no longer, so take yourself off out of my
stable; I shall not take you back again until you are stronger
than a lion.' Then he opened the door and turned him adrift.

The poor horse was very melancholy and wandered up and
down in the wood, seeking some little shelter from the cold
wind and rain. Presently a fox met him: 'What's the
matter, my friend?' said he, 'why do you hang down your
head and look so lonely and woebegone?' 'Ah!' replied

105

the horse, 'justice and avarice never dwell in one house; my master has forgotten all that I have done for him so many years, and because I can no longer work he has turned me adrift, and says unless I become stronger than a lion he will not take me back again; what chance can I have of that? He knows I have none, or he would not talk so.'

However, the fox bid him be of good cheer and said: 'I will help you; lie down there, stretch yourself out quite stiff, and pretend to be dead.' The horse did as he was told, and the fox went straight to the lion who lived in a cave close by, and said to him: 'A little way off lies a dead horse; come with me and you may make an excellent meal of his carcass.' The lion was greatly pleased, and set off immediately; and when they came to the horse, the fox said: 'You will not be able to eat him comfortably here; I 'll tell you what—I will tie you fast to his tail, and then you can draw him to your den, and eat him at your leisure.'

This advice pleased the lion, so he laid himself down quietly for the fox to make him fast to the horse. But the fox managed to tie his legs together and bound all so hard and fast that with all his strength he could not set himself free. When the work was done, the fox clapped the horse on the shoulder and said: 'Jip! Dobbin! Jip!' Then up he sprang, and moved off, dragging the lion behind him. The beast began to roar and bellow, till all the birds of the wood flew away for fright; but the horse let him sing on, and made his way quietly over the fields to his master's house.

'Here he is, master,' said he, 'I have got the better of him.' And when the farmer saw his old servant, his heart relented, and he said: 'Thou shalt stay in thy stable and be well taken care of.' And so the poor old horse had plenty to eat, and lived—till he died.

# The Travelling Musicians

AN honest farmer had once an ass that had been a faithful servant to him a great many years, but was now growing old and every day more and more unfit for work. His master therefore was tired of keeping him and began to think of putting an end to him; but the ass, who saw that some mischief was in the wind, took himself slyly off, and began his journey towards the great city, 'for there,' thought he, 'I may turn musician.'

After he had travelled a little way, he spied a dog lying by the roadside and panting as if he were very tired. 'What makes you pant so, my friend?' said the ass. 'Alas!' said the dog, 'my master was going to knock me on the head, because I am old and weak, and can no longer make myself useful to him in hunting; so I ran away; but what can I do to earn my livelihood?' 'Hark ye!' said the ass, 'I am going to the great city to turn musician; suppose you go with me, and try what you can do in the same way?' The dog said he was willing, and they jogged on together.

They had not gone far before they saw a cat sitting in the middle of the road and making a most rueful face. 'Pray, my good lady,' said the ass, 'what's the matter with you? you look quite out of spirits!' 'Ah me!' said the cat. 'How can one be in good spirits when one's life is in danger? Because I am beginning to grow old, and had rather lie down at my ease by the fire than run about the house after the mice, my mistress laid hold of me, and was going to drown me; and though I have been lucky enough to get away from her, I do not know what I am to live upon.' 'Oh!' said the ass, 'by all means go with us to the great city; you are a good night singer, and may make your fortune as a musician.' The cat was pleased with the thought, and joined the party.

Soon afterwards, as they were passing by a farmyard, they saw a cock perched upon a gate, and crowing away with all his might and main. 'Bravo!' said the ass; 'upon my word you make a famous noise; pray what is all this about?' 'Why,' said the cock, 'I was just now saying that we should have fine weather for our washing-day, and yet my mistress and the cook don't thank me for my pains, but threaten to cut off my head to-morrow, and make broth of me for the guests that are coming on Sunday!' 'Heaven forbid!' said the ass; 'come with us, Master Chanticleer; it will be better, at any rate, than staying here to have your head cut off! Besides, who knows? If we care to sing in tune, we may get up some kind of a concert: so come along with us.' 'With all my heart!' said the cock: so they all four went on jollily together.

They could not, however, reach the great city the first day; so when night came on they went into a wood to sleep. The ass and the dog laid themselves down under a great tree, and the cat climbed up into the branches; while the cock, thinking that the higher he sat the safer he would be, flew up to the very top of the tree, and then, according to his custom, before he went to sleep, looked out on all sides of him to see that everything was well. In doing this, he saw afar off something bright and shining; and calling to his companions said: 'There must be a house no great way off, for I see a light.' 'If that be the case,' said the ass, 'we had better change our quarters, for our lodging is not the best in the world!' 'Besides,' added the dog, 'I should not be the worse for a bone or two, or a bit of meat.' So they walked off together towards the spot where Chanticleer had seen the light; and as they drew near, it became larger and brighter, till they at last came close to a house in which a gang of robbers lived.

The ass, being the tallest of the company, marched up to the window and peeped in. 'Well, Donkey,' said Chanticleer, 'what do you see?' 'What do I see?' replied the ass, 'why I see a table spread with all kinds of good things, and robbers sitting round it making merry.' 'That would be a noble lodging for us,' said the cock. 'Yes' said the

ass, 'if we could only get in': so they consulted together
how they should contrive to get the robbers out; and at
last they hit upon a plan.  The ass placed himself upright
on his hind legs, with his forefeet resting against the
window; the dog got upon his back; the cat scrambled
up to the dog's shoulders, and the cock flew up and sat
upon the cat's head.  When all was ready, a signal was
given, and they began their music.  The ass brayed, the
dog barked, the cat mewed, and the cock crowed; and
then they all broke through the window at once, and came
tumbling into the room, amongst the broken glass, with a
most hideous clatter!  The robbers, who had been not a
little frightened by the opening concert, had now no doubt
that some frightful hobgoblin had broken in upon them, and
scampered away as fast as they could.

The coast once clear, our travellers soon sat down, and
dispatched what the robbers had left, with as much eager-
ness as if they had not expected to eat again for a month.
As soon as they had satisfied themselves, they put out the
lights, and each once more sought out a resting-place to his
own liking.  The donkey laid himself down upon a heap of
straw in the yard; the dog stretched himself upon a mat
behind the door; the cat rolled herself up on the hearth
before the warm ashes; and the cock perched upon a
beam on the top of the house; and, as they were all rather
tired with their journey, they soon fell asleep.

But about midnight, when the robbers saw from afar that
the lights were out and that all seemed quiet, they began to
think that they had been in too great a hurry to run away;
and one of them, who was bolder than the rest, went to see
what was going on.  Finding everything still, he marched
into the kitchen, and groped about till he found a match
in order to light a candle; and then, espying the glittering

fiery eyes of the cat, he mistook them for live coals, and held the match to them to light it. But the cat, not understanding this joke, sprung at his face, and spat and scratched at him. This frightened him dreadfully, and away he ran to the back door; but there the dog jumped up and bit him in the leg; and as he was crossing over the yard the ass kicked him; and the cock, who had been awakened by the noise, crowed with all his might. At this the robber ran back as fast as he could to his comrades, and told the captain how a horrid witch had got into the house, and had spit at him and scratched his face with her long bony fingers; how a man with a knife in his hand had hidden himself behind the door, and stabbed him in the leg; how a black monster stood in the yard and struck him with a club, and how the devil had sat upon the top of the house and cried out: 'Throw the rascal up here!' After this the robbers never dared to go back to the house; but the musicians were so pleased with their quarters that they took up their abode there; and there they are, I dare say, at this very day.

# The Golden Goose

THERE was a man who had three sons. The youngest
was called Dummling—which is much the same as
Dunderhead, for all thought he was more than half a fool—
and he was at all times mocked and ill-treated by the whole
household.

It happened that the eldest son took it into his head
one day to go into the wood to cut fuel; and his mother
gave him a nice pasty and a bottle of wine to take with
him, that he might refresh himself at his work. As he
went into the wood, a little old man bade him good day
and said: 'Give me a little piece of meat from your plate, and
a little wine out of your bottle, for I am very hungry

and thirsty.' But this clever young man said: 'Give you my meat and wine? No, I thank you, I should not have enough left for myself': and away he went. He soon began to cut down a tree; but he had not worked long before he missed his stroke, and cut himself, and was forced to go home to have the wound dressed. Now it was the little old man that sent him this mischief.

Next the second son went out to work: and his mother gave him too a pasty and a bottle of wine. And the same little old man met him also, and asked him for something to eat and drink. But he too thought himself very clever, and said: 'The more you eat the less there would be for me; so go your way!' The little man took care that he too should have his reward, and the second stroke that he aimed against the tree hit him on the leg; so that he too was forced to go home.

Then Dummling said: 'Father, I should like to go and cut wood too.' But his father said: 'Your brothers have both lamed themselves; you had better stay at home, for you know nothing about the business of wood-cutting.' But Dummling was very pressing; and at last his father said, 'Go your way! You will be wiser when you have smarted for your folly.' And his mother gave him only some dry bread and a bottle of sour beer. But when he went into the wood, he met the little old man, who said: 'Give me some meat and drink, for I am very hungry and thirsty.' Dummling said: 'I have only dry bread and sour beer; if that will suit you we will sit down and eat it, such as it is, together.' So they sat down; and when the lad pulled out his bread behold it was turned into a rich pasty, and his sour beer, when they tasted it, was delightful wine. They ate and drank heartily; and when they had done, the little man said: 'As you have a kind heart, and have been willing to share everything with me, I will send a blessing upon you. There stands an old tree; cut it down, and you will find something at the root.' Then he took his leave and went his way.

Dummling set to work and cut down the tree, and when it fell he found, in a hollow under the roots, a goose with feathers of pure gold. He took it up, and went on to a little inn by the roadside, where he thought to sleep for the night on his way home. Now the landlord had three daughters; and when they saw the goose they were very eager to see what this wonderful bird could be, and wished very much to pluck one of the feathers our of its tail. At last the eldest said: 'I must and will have a feather.' So she waited till Dummling was gone to bed, and then seized the goose by the wing; but to her great wonder there she stuck, for neither hand nor finger could she get away again. Then in came the second sister, and thought to have a feather too; but the moment she touched her sister, there she too hung fast. At last came the third, and she also wanted a feather; but the other two cried out: 'Keep away! For Heaven's sake, keep away!' However, she did not understand what they meant. 'If they are there,' thought she, 'I may as well be there too.' So she went up to them; but the moment she touched her sisters she stuck fast, and hung to the goose, as they did. And so they kept company with the goose all night in the cold.

The next morning Dummling got up and carried off the goose under his arm. He took no notice at all of the three girls, but went out with them sticking fast behind. So wherever he travelled, they too were forced to follow, whether they would or no, as fast as their legs could carry them.

In the middle of a field the parson met them; and when he saw the train, he said: 'Are you not ashamed of yourselves, you bold girls, to run after a young man in that way over the fields? Is that good behaviour?' Then he took the youngest by the hand to lead her away; but as soon as he touched her he too hung fast, and followed in the train; though sorely against his will, for he was not only in rather too good plight for running fast, but just then he had a little touch of the gout in the great toe of his right foot. By and by up came the clerk; and when he saw his master, the parson, running after the three girls, he wondered greatly and said: 'Hallo! hallo! your reverence! whither so fast? There is a christening to-day.' Then he ran up and took him by the gown; when, lo and behold, he stuck fast too. As the five were thus trudging along, one behind another, they met two labourers with their mattocks coming from work; and the parson cried out lustily to them to help him. But scarcely had they laid hands on him, when they too fell into the rank; and so they made seven, all running together after Dummling and his goose.

Now Dummling thought he would see a little of the world before he went home; so he and his train journeyed on, till at last they came to a city where there was a king who had an only daughter. The princess was of so thoughtful and moody a turn of mind that no one could make her laugh; and the king had made known to all the world, that whoever could make her laugh should have her for his wife. When the young man heard this, he went to her, with his goose and all its train; and as soon as she saw the seven all hanging together, and running along, treading on each other's heels, she could not help bursting into a long and loud laugh. Then Dummling claimed her for his wife, and married her; and he was heir to the kingdom, and lived long and happily with his wife.

But what became of the goose and the goose's tail I never could hear.

# The Wishing Table

A LONG time ago there lived a tailor who had three sons but only one goat. As the goat supplied the whole family with milk, she had to be well fed and taken daily to pasture. This the sons did in turn. One day the eldest son led her into the churchyard, where he knew there was fine herbage to be found, and there let her browse and skip about till evening. It being then time to return home, he said to her: 'Goat, have you had enough to eat?' and the goat answered:

> 'I have eaten so much
> Not a leaf can I touch. Nan. Nan.'

'Come along home then,' said the boy, and he led her by the cord round her neck back to the stable and tied her up.

'Well,' said the old tailor, 'has the goat had her proper amount of food?'

'Why, she has eaten so much, not a leaf can she touch,' answered the son.

The father, however, thinking he should like to assure himself of this, went down to the stable, patted the animal, and said caressingly: 'Goat, have you really had enough to eat?' The goat answered:

> 'How can my hunger be allayed?
> About the little graves I played
> And could not find a single blade.    Nan.   Nan.'

'What is this I hear!' cried the tailor, and running upstairs to his son, 'You young liar!' he exclaimed, 'to tell me the goat had had enough to eat, and all the while she is starving.' And overcome with anger, he took his yard-measure down from the wall and beat his son out of doors.

The next day it was the second son's turn, and he found a place near a garden hedge, where there were the juiciest plants for the goats to feed upon, and she enjoyed them so much that she ate them all up. Before taking her home in the evening, he said to her: 'Goat, have you had enough to eat?' and the goat answered:

> 'I have eaten so much
> Not a leaf can I touch.    Nan.   Nan.'

'Come along home then,' said the boy, and he led her away to the stable and tied her up.

'Well,' said the old tailor, 'has the goat had her proper amount of food?'

'Why, she has eaten so much, not a leaf can she touch,' answered the boy.

But the tailor was not satisfied with this, and went down

to the stable. 'Goat, have you really had enough to eat?'
he asked; and the goat answered:

> 'How can my hunger be allayed?
> About the little graves I played
> And could not find a single blade. Nan. Nan.'

'The shameless young rascal!', cried the tailor, 'to let
an innocent animal like this starve!' and he ran upstairs,
and drove the boy from the house with the yard-measure.

It was now the third son's turn, who, hoping to make
things better for himself, let the goat feed on the leaves of
all the shrubs he could pick out that were covered with the
richest foliage. 'Goat, have you had enough to eat?' he
said, as the evening fell, and the goat answered:

> 'I have eaten so much
> Not a leaf can I touch. Nan. Nan.'

'Come along home then,' said the boy, and he took her
back and tied her up.

'Well,' said the old tailor, 'has the goat had her proper
amount of food?'

'Why, she has eaten so much, not a leaf can she touch,'
answered the boy.

But the tailor felt mistrustful, and went down and asked:
'Goat, have you really had enough to eat?' and the mis-
chievous animal answered:

> 'How can my hunger be allayed?
> About the little graves I played
> And could not find a single blade. Nan. Nan.'

'Oh, what a pack of liars!' cried the tailor. 'One
as wicked and deceitful as the other, but they shall not
make a fool of me any longer.' And beside himself with
anger, he rushed upstairs, and so belaboured his son with
the yard-measure, that the boy fled from the house.

The old tailor was now left alone with his goat. The following morning he went down to the stable and stroked and caressed her. 'Come along, my pet,' he said, 'I will take you out myself to-day,' and he led her by the green hedgerows and weed-grown banks, and wherever he knew that goats love to feed. 'You shall eat to your heart's content for once,' he said to her, and so let her browse till evening. 'Goat, have you had enough to eat?' he asked her at the close of day, and she answered:

> 'I have eaten so much
> Not a leaf can I touch. Nan. Nan.'

'Come along home then,' said the tailor, and he led her to the stable and tied her up. He turned round, however, before leaving her, and said once more: 'You have really had enough to eat for once?' But the goat gave him no better answer than her usual one, and replied:

> 'How can my hunger be allayed?
> About the little graves I played
> And could not find a single blade. Nan. Nan.'

On hearing this, the tailor stood, struck dumb with astonishment. He saw how unjust he had been in driving away his sons. When he found his voice, he cried: 'Wait, you ungrateful creature! it is not enough to drive you away, but I will put such a mark upon you, that you will not dare to show your face again among honest tailors.' And so saying, he sprang upstairs, brought down his razor, lathered the goat's head all over, and shaved it till it was as smooth as the back of his hand. Then he fetched the whip—his yard-measure he considered was too good for such work— and dealt the animal such blows, that she leapt into the air and away.

Sitting now quite alone in his house, the tailor fell into great melancholy, and would gladly have had his sons back again, but no one knew what had become of them.

The eldest had apprenticed himself to a joiner, and had set himself cheerfully and diligently to learn his trade. When the time came for him to start as a journeyman, his master made him a present of a table, which was of ordinary wood, and to all outward appearance exactly like any other table. It had, however, one good quality, for if any one set it down, and said: 'Table, serve up a meal,' it was immediately covered with a nice fresh cloth, laid with a plate, knife and fork, and dishes of boiled and baked meats, as many as there was room for, and a glass of red wine, which only to look at made the heart rejoice.

'I have enough now to last me as long as I live,' thought the young man to himself, and accordingly he went about enjoying himself, nor minding whether the inns he stayed at were good or bad, whether there was food to be had there or not. Sometimes it pleased him not to seek shelter within them at all, but to turn into a field or a wood, or wherever else he fancied. When there he put down his table, and said: 'Serve up a meal,' and he was at once supplied with everything he could desire in the way of food.

After he had been going about like this for some time, he bethought him that he should like to go home again. His father's anger would by this time have passed away, and now that he had the wishing-table with him, he was sure of a ready welcome.

He happened, on his homeward way, to come one evening to an inn full of guests. They bade him welcome, and invited him to sit down with them and share their supper, otherwise, they added, he would have a difficulty in getting anything to eat.

But the joiner replied: 'I will not take from you what little you have, I would rather that you should consent to be my guests,' whereupon they all laughed, thinking he was only joking with them. He now put down his table in the middle of the room, and said, 'Table, serve up a meal,' and in a moment it was covered with a variety of food of better quality than any the host could have supplied, and a fragrant steam rose from the dishes and greeted the nostrils of the guests. 'Now friends, fall to,' said the young man, and the guests, seeing that the invitation was well intended, did not wait to be asked twice, but drew up their chairs and began vigorously to ply their knives and forks. What astonished them most was the way in which, as soon as a dish was empty, another full one appeared in its place. Meanwhile the landlord was standing in the corner of the room looking on; he did not know what to think of it all, but said to himself: 'I could make good use of a cook like that.'

The joiner and his friends kept up their merriment late into the night, but at last they retired to rest, the young journeyman placing his table against the wall before going to bed.

The landlord, however, could not sleep for thinking of what he had seen; at last it occurred to him that up in his lumber-room he had an old table, which was just such another one to all appearance as the wishing-table; so he crept away softly to fetch it, and put it against the wall in place of the other.

When the morning came, the joiner paid for his night's lodging, took up his table, and left, never suspecting that the one he was carrying was not his own.

He reached home at midday, and was greeted with joy by his father. 'And now, dear son,' said the old man, 'what trade have you learnt?'

'I am a joiner, father.'

'A capital business,' responded the father, 'and what have you brought home with you from your travels?'

'The best thing I have brought with me, father, is that table.'

The tailor carefully examined the table on all sides. 'Well,' he said at last, 'you have certainly not brought a masterpiece back with you; it is a wretched, badly made old table.'

'But it is a wishing-table,' interrupted his son. 'If I put it down and order a meal, it is at once covered with the best of food and wine. If you will only invite your relations and friends, they shall, for once in their lives, have a good meal, for no one ever leaves this table unsatisfied.'

When the guests were assembled, he put his table down as usual and said, 'Table, serve up a meal,' but the table did not stir, and remained as empty as any ordinary table at such a command. Then the poor young man saw that his table had been changed, and he was covered with shame at having to stand there before them all like a liar. The guests made fun of him, and had to return home without bite or sup. The tailor took out his cloth and sat down once more to his tailoring, and the son started work again under a master-joiner.

The second son had apprenticed himself to a miller. When his term of apprenticeship had expired, the miller said to him: 'As you have behaved so well, I will make you a present of an ass; it is a curious animal, it will neither draw a cart nor carry a sack.'

'Of what use is he then?' asked the young apprentice. 'He gives gold,' answered the miller, 'if you stand him on a cloth, and say "Bricklebrit," gold pieces will fall from his mouth.

'That is a handsome present,' said the young miller, and he thanked his master and departed.

After this, whenever he was in need of money, he had only to say 'Bricklebrit,' and a shower of gold pieces fell on the ground, and all he had to do was to pick them up. He ordered the best of everything wherever he went, in short, the dearer the better, for his purse was always full.

He had been going about the world like this for some time, when he began to think he should like to see his father again. 'When he sees my gold ass,' he said to himself, 'he will forget his anger, and be glad to have me back.'

It came to pass that he arrived one evening at the same inn in which his brother had had his table stolen from him. He was leading his ass up to the door, when the landlord came out and offered to take the animal, but the young miller refused his help. 'Do not trouble yourself,' he said, 'I will take my old Greycoat myself to the stable and fasten her up, as I like to know where she is.'

The landlord was very much astonished at this; the man cannot be very well off, he thought, to look after his own ass. When the stranger, therefore, pulled two gold pieces out of his pocket, and ordered the best of everything that could be got in the market, the landlord opened his eyes, but he ran off with alacrity to do his bidding.

Having finished his meal, the stranger asked for his bill, and the landlord thinking he might safely overcharge such a rich customer, asked for two more gold pieces. The miller felt in his pocket but found he had spent all his gold. 'Wait a minute,' he said to the landlord, 'I will go and fetch some more money.' Whereupon he went out, carrying the table-cloth with him.

This was more than the landlord's curiosity could stand, and he followed his guest to the stable. As the latter bolted the door after him, he went and peeped through a hole in the wall, and there he saw the stranger spread the cloth under his ass, and heard him say, 'Bricklebrit,' and immediately the floor was covered with gold pieces which fell from the animal's mouth.

'A good thousand, I declare,' cried the host, 'the gold pieces do not take long to coin! It 's not a bad thing to have a money-bag like that.'

The guest settled his account and went to bed. During the night the landlord crept down to the stable, led away the gold-coining ass, and fastened up another in its place.

Early the next morning the young miller went off with the ass, thinking all the time that he was leading his own. By noonday he had reached home, where his father gave him a warm welcome.

'What have you been doing with yourself, my son?' asked the old man.

'I am a miller, dear father,' he answered.

'And what have you brought home with you from your travels?'

'Nothing but an ass, father.'

'There are asses enough here,' said the father, 'I should have been better pleased if it had been a goat.'

'Very likely,' replied the son, 'but this is no ordinary ass, it is an ass that coins money; if I say "Bricklebrit" to it, a whole sackful of gold pours from its mouth. Call all your relations and friends together, I will turn you all into rich people.'

'I shall like that well enough,' said the tailor, 'for then I shall not have to go on plaguing myself with stitching,' and he ran out himself to invite his neighbours. As soon as they were all assembled, the young miller asked them to clear a space, and then he spread his cloth and brought the ass into the room. 'Now see,' said he, and cried 'Bricklebrit,' but not a single gold piece appeared, and it was evident that the animal knew nothing of the art of gold-coining, for it is not every ass that attains to such a degree of excellence.

The poor young miller pulled a long face, for he saw that he had been tricked: he begged forgiveness of the company, who all returned home as poor as they came. There is nothing to be done now but for the old man to go back to his needle, and the young one to hire himself to a miller.

The third son had apprenticed himself to a turner, which, being a trade requiring a great deal of skill, obliged him to serve a longer time than his brothers. He had, however, heard from them by letter, and knew how badly things had gone with them, and that they had been robbed of their property by an innkeeper on the last evening before reaching home.

When it was time for him to start as a journeyman, his master, being pleased with his conduct, presented him with a bag, saying as he did so: 'You will find a cudgel inside.'

'The bag I can carry over my shoulder, and it will no doubt be of great service to me, but of what use is a cudgel inside, it will only add to the weight?'

'I will explain,' said the master. 'If any one at any time should behave badly to you, you have only to say: "Cudgel, out of the bag," and the stick will jump out, and give him such a cudgelling, that he will not be able to move or stir for a week afterwards, and it will not leave off till you say: "Cudgel, into the bag."'

The young man thanked him, hung the bag on his back, and when any one threatened to attack him, or in any way to do him harm, he called out: 'Cudgel, out of the bag,' and no sooner were the words said than out jumped the stick, and beat the offenders soundly on the back, till their clothes were in ribbons, and it did it all so quickly, that the turn had come round to each of them before he was aware.

It was evening when the young turner reached the inn where his brothers had been so badly treated. He laid his bag down on the table, and began giving an account of all the wonderful things he had seen while going about the world.

'One may come across a wishing-table,' he said, 'or an ass that gives gold, and such like; all very good things in their way, but not all of them put together are worth the treasure of which I have possession, and which I carry with me in that bag.'

The landlord pricked up his ears. 'What can it be?' he asked himself, 'the bag must be filled with precious stones; I must try and get hold of that cheaply too, for there is luck in odd numbers.'

Bed-time came, and the guest stretched himself out on one of the benches and placed his bag under his head for a pillow. As soon as the landlord thought he was fast asleep, he went up to him, and began gently and cautiously pulling and pushing at the bag to see if he could get it away and put another in its place.

But the young miller had been waiting for this and just as the landlord was about to give a good last pull, he cried: 'Cudgel, out of the bag,' and the same moment the stick was out, and beginning its usual dance. It beat him with such a vengeance that the landlord cried out for mercy. but the louder his cries, the more lustily did the stick beat time to them, until he fell to the ground exhausted.

'If you do not give back the wishing-table and the gold ass,' said the young turner, 'the game shall begin over again.'

'No, no,' cried the landlord in a feeble voice, 'I will gladly give everything back, if only you will make that dreadful demon of a stick return to the bag.'

'This time,' said the turner, 'I will deal with you according to mercy rather than justice, but beware of offending in like manner again.'   Then he cried: 'Cudgel, into the bag,' and let the man remain in peace.

The turner journeyed on next day to his father's house, taking with him the wishing-table and the gold ass.   The tailor was delighted to see his son again, and asked him, as he had the others, what trade he had learnt since he left home.

'I am a turner, dear father,' he answered.

'A highly skilled trade,' said the tailor, 'and what have you brought back with you from your travels?'

'An invaluable thing, dear father,' said the son, 'a cudgel.'

'What! a cudgel!' exclaimed the old man, 'that was certainly worth while, seeing that you can cut yourself one from the first tree you come across.'

'But not such a one as this, dear father; for, if I say to it, 'Cudgel, out of the bag,' out it jumps, and gives any one who has evil intentions towards me such a bad time of it, that he falls down and cries for mercy.   And know, that it was with this stick that I got back the wishing-table and the gold ass, which the dishonest inn-keeper stole from my brothers.   Now, go and call them both here, and invite all your relations and friends, and I will feast them and fill their pockets with gold.'

The old tailor was slow to believe all this, but nevertheless he went out and gathered his neighbours together. Then the turner put down a cloth, and led in the gold ass, and said to his brother: 'Now, dear brother, speak to him.'

The miller said, 'Bricklebrit,' and the cloth was immediately covered with gold pieces, which continued to pour from the ass's mouth until every one had taken as many as he could carry. (I see by your faces that you are all wishing you had been there.)

Then the turner brought in the wishing-table, and said: 'Now, dear brother, speak to it.' And scarcely had the joiner cried, 'Table, serve up a meal,' than it was covered with a profusion of daintily dressed meats. Then the tailor and his guests sat down to a meal such as they had never enjoyed before in all their lives, and they all sat up late into the night, full of good cheer and jollity.

The tailor put away his needle and thread, his yard-measure, and his goose, and he and his three sons lived together henceforth in contentment and luxury.

Meanwhile, what had become of the goat, who had been the guilty cause of the three sons being driven from their home? I will tell you.

She was so ashamed of her shaven crown, that she ran and crept into a fox's hole. When the fox came home, he was met by two large glittering eyes that gleamed at him out of the darkness, and he was so frightened that he ran away. The bear met him, and perceiving that he was in some distress, said: 'What is the matter, brother Fox, why are you pulling such a long face?' 'Ah!' answered Redskin, 'there is a dreadful animal sitting in my hole, which glared at me with fiery eyes.'

'We will soon drive him out,' said the bear, and he trotted back with his friend to the hole and looked in, but the sight of the fiery eyes was quite enough for him, and he turned and took to his heels.

The bee met him and noticing that he was somewhat ill at ease, said: 'Bear, you look remarkably out of humour, where have you left your good spirits?' 'It's easy for you to talk,' replied the bear, 'a horrible animal with red goggle-eyes is sitting in the fox's hole, and we cannot drive it out.'

The bee said: 'I really am sorry for you, Bear; I am but a poor weak little creature that you scarcely deign to look at in passing, but, for all that, I think I shall be able to help you.'

With this the bee flew to the fox's hole, settled on the smooth shaven head of the goat, and stung her so violently, that she leaped high into the air, crying, 'Nan, nan!' and fled away like a mad thing into the open country; but no one, to this hour, has found out what became of her after that.

# Tom Thumb

A POOR woodman sat in his cottage one night, smoking his pipe by the fireside, while his wife sat by his side spinning. 'How lonely it is, wife,' said he, as he puffed out a long curl of smoke, 'for you and me to sit here by ourselves, without any children to play about and amuse us, while other people seem so happy and merry with their children!' 'What you say is very true,' said the wife, sighing, and turning round her wheel; 'how happy should I be if I had but one child! If it were ever so small—nay, if it were no bigger than my thumb—I should be very happy, and love it dearly.' Now—odd as you may think it—it came to pass that this good woman's wish was fulfilled, just in the very way she had wished it; for, not long afterwards, she had a little boy, who was quite healthy and strong, but was not much bigger than my thumb. So they said: 'Well, we cannot say we have not got what we wished for, and, little as he is, we will love him dearly.' And they called him Thomas Thumb.

They gave him plenty of food, yet for all they could do he never grew bigger, but kept just the same size as he had been when he was born. Still, his eyes were sharp and sparkling, and he soon showed himself to be a clever little fellow, who always knew well what he was about.

One day, as the woodman was getting ready to go into the wood to cut fuel, he said: 'I wish I had someone to bring the cart after me, for I want to make haste.' 'Oh, father,' cried Tom, 'I will take care of that; the cart shall be in the wood by the time you want it.' Then the woodman laughed, and said: 'How can that be? You cannot reach up to the horse's bridle.' 'Never mind that, father,' said Tom; 'if my mother will only harness the horse, I will get into his ear and tell him which way to go.' 'Well,' said his father, 'we will try for once.'

When the time came the mother harnessed the horse to the cart, and put Tom into his ear; and as he sat there the little man told the beast how to go, crying out, 'Go on!' and 'Stop!' as he wanted: and thus the horse went on just as well as if the woodman had driven it himself into the wood. It happened that as the horse was going a little too fast, and Tom was calling out, 'Gently! gently!' two strangers came up. 'What an odd thing that is!' said one; 'there is a cart going along, and I hear a carter talking to the horse, but yet I see no one.' 'That is queer, indeed,' said the other; 'let us follow the cart, and see where it goes.' So they went on into the wood, till at last they came to the place where the woodman was. Then Tom Thumb, seeing his father, cried out: 'See, father, here I am with the cart, all right and safe! now take me down!' So his father took hold of the horse with one hand, and with the other took his son out of the horse's ear, and put him down upon the straw, where he sat as merry as you please.

The two strangers were all this time looking on, and did not know what to say for wonder. At last one took the other aside, and said: 'That little urchin will make our fortune, if we can get him, and carry him about from town to town as a show: we must buy him.' So they went up to the woodman, and asked him what he would take for the little man; 'He will be better off,' said they, 'with us than with you.' 'I won't sell him at all,' said the father; 'my own flesh and blood is dearer to me than all the silver and gold in the world.' But Tom, hearing of the bargain they wanted to make, crept up his father's coat to his shoulder, and whispered in his ear: 'Take the money, father, and let them have me; I 'll soon come back to you.'

So the woodman at last said that he would sell Tom to the strangers for a large piece of gold, and they paid the price. 'Where would you like to sit?' said one of them. 'Oh, put me on the brim of your hat; that will be a nice gallery for me; I can walk about there, and see the country as we go along.' So they did as he wished; and when Tom had taken leave of his father they took him away with them.

They journeyed on till it began to grow dusk, and then the little man said: 'Let me get down, I 'm tired.' So the man took off his hat, and put him down on a clod of earth, in a ploughed field by the side of the road. But Tom ran about amongst the furrows, and at last slipped into an old mouse-hole. 'Good night, my masters!' said he, 'I 'm off! mind and look sharp after me the next time.' Then they ran at once to the place, and poked the ends of their sticks into the mouse-hole, but all in vain; Tom only crawled farther and farther in; and at last it became quite dark, so that they were forced to go their way without their prize, as sulky as could be.

When Tom found they were gone, he came out of his hiding-place. 'What dangerous walking it is,' said he, 'in this ploughed field! If I were to fall from one of these great clods, I should undoubtedly break my neck.' At last, by good luck, he found a large empty snail-shell. 'This is lucky,' said he, 'I can sleep here very well'; and in he crept.

Just as he was falling aleep, he heard two men passing by, chatting together; and one said to the other: 'How can we rob that rich parson's house of his silver and gold?' 'I 'll tell you,' cried Tom. 'What noise was that?' said the thief, frightened; 'I 'm sure I heard someone speak.' They stood still listening, and Tom said: 'Take me with you, and I 'll soon show you how to get the parson's money.' 'But where are you?' said they. 'Look about on the ground,' answered he, 'and listen where the sound comes from.' At last the thieves found him out, and lifted him up in their hands. 'You little urchin!' they said, 'what can you do for us?' 'Why I can get between the iron window-bars of the parson's house and throw you out whatever you want.' 'That 's a good thought,' said the thieves; 'come along, we shall see what you can do.'

When they came to the parson's house, Tom slipped through the window-bars into the room, and then called out as loud as he could bawl: 'Will you have all that is here?' At this the thieves were frightened, and said: 'Softly, softly! speak low, that you may not awaken anybody.' But Tom seemed as if he did not understand them, and bawled out again: 'How much will you have? shall I throw it all out?' Now the cook lay in the next room; and hearing a noise she raised herself up in her bed and listened. Meantime the thieves were frightened, and ran off a little way; but at last they plucked up their hearts, and said: 'The little urchin is only trying to make fools of us.' So they came back and whispered softly to him, saying: 'Now let us have no more of your roguish jokes; but throw us out some of the money.' Then Tom called out as loud as he could: 'Very well! hold your hands! here it comes.'

The cook heard this quite plain, so she sprang out of bed, and ran to open the door. The thieves ran off as if a wolf was at their tails; and the maid, having groped about and found nothing, went away for a light. By the time she came back, Tom had slipped off into the barn; and when she had looked about and searched every hole and corner, and found nobody, she went to bed, thinking she must have been dreaming with her eyes open.

The little man crawled about in the hay-loft, and at last found a snug place to finish his night's rest in; so he laid himself down, meaning to sleep till daylight, and then find his way home to his father and mother. But alas! how woefully was he undone! what crosses and sorrows happen to us all in this world! The cook got up early, before daybreak, to feed the cows; and going straight to the hay-loft, carried away a large bundle of hay, with the little man in the middle of it, fast asleep. He still, however, slept on, and did not awake till he found himself in the mouth of the cow; for the cook had put the hay into the cow's rack, and the cow had taken Tom up in a mouthful of it. 'Good lack-a-day!' said he, 'how came I to tumble into the mill?' But he soon found out where he really was; and was forced to have all his wits about him, that he might not get between the cow's teeth, and so be crushed to death. At last down he went into her stomach. 'It is rather dark here,' said he; they forgot to build windows in this room to let the sun in; a candle would be no bad thing.'

Though he made the best of his bad luck, he did not like his quarters at all; and the worst of it was, that more and more hay was always coming down, and the space left for him became smaller and smaller. At last he cried out as loud as he could: 'Don't bring me any more hay! Don't bring me any more hay!'

The maid happened just then to be milking the cow; and hearing someone speak, but seeing nobody, and yet being quite sure it was the same voice that she had heard in the night, she was so frightened that she fell off her stool, and overset the milk-pail. As soon as she could pick herself up out of the dirt, she ran off as fast as she could to her master the parson, and said: 'Sir, sir, the cow is talking!' But the parson said: 'Woman, thou art surely mad!' However, he went with her into the cow-house, to try and see what was the matter.

Scarcely had they set their foot on the threshold, when Tom called out: 'Don't bring me any more hay!' Then the parson himself was frightened; and thinking the cow was surely bewitched, told his man to kill her on the spot. So the cow was killed, and cut up; and the stomach, in which Tom lay, was thrown out upon a dunghill.

Tom soon set himself to work to get out, which was not a very easy task; but at last, just as he had made room to get his head out, fresh ill-luck befell him. A hungry wolf sprang out, and swallowed up the whole stomach, with Tom in it, at one gulp, and ran away.

Tom, however, was still not disheartened; and thinking the wolf would not dislike having some chat with him as he was going along, he called out: 'My good friend, I can show you a famous treat.' 'Where's that?' said the wolf. 'In such and such a house,' said Tom, describing his own father's house: 'you can crawl through the drain into the kitchen, and then into the pantry, and there you will find cakes, ham, beef, cold chicken, roast pig, apple dumplings, and everything that your heart can wish.'

The wolf did not want to be asked twice; so that very night he went to the house and crawled through the drain into the kitchen, and then into the pantry, and ate and drank there to his heart's content. As soon as he had had enough he wanted to get away; but he had eaten so much that he could not go out by the same way that he came in.

This was just what Tom had reckoned upon; and now he began to set up a great shout, making all the noise he could. 'Will you be easy?' said the wolf: 'you'll waken everybody in the house if you make such a clatter.' 'What's that to me?' said the little man: 'you have had your frolic, now I've a mind to be merry myself'; and he began again, singing and shouting as loud as he could.

The woodman and his wife being awakened by the noise, peeped through a crack in the door; but when they saw that the wolf was there, you may well suppose that they were sadly frightened; and the woodman ran for his axe, and gave his wife a scythe. 'Do you stay behind,' said the woodman, 'and when I have knocked him on the head you must rip him up with the scythe.' Tom heard all this said, and cried out: 'Father, father! I am here, the wolf has swallowed me.' And his father said: 'Heaven be praised! we have found our dear child again'; and he told his wife not to use the scythe for fear she should hurt him. Then he aimed a great blow, and struck the wolf on the head, and killed him on the spot; and when he was dead they cut open his body, and set Tommy free. 'Ah!' said the father, 'what fears we have had for you!' 'Yes, father,' answered he: 'I have travelled all over the world, I think, in one way or other, since we parted; and now I am very glad to come home and get fresh air again.' 'Why, where have you been?' said his father. 'I have been in a mouse-hole,—and in a snail-shell,—and down a cow's throat,—and in the wolf's belly; and yet here I am again, safe and sound.'

'Well,' said they, 'you are come back, and we will not sell you again for all the riches in the world.'

Then they hugged and kissed their dear little son, and gave him plenty to eat and drink, for he was very hungry; and then they fetched new clothes for him for his old ones had been quite spoiled on his journey. So Master Thumb stayed at home with his father and mother, in peace; for though he had been so great a traveller, and had done and seen so many fine things, and was fond enough of telling the whole story, he always agreed that, after all,—There's no place like HOME!

# Snow White

IT was the middle of winter, when the broad flakes of snow were falling around, that the queen of a country many thousand miles off sat working at her window. The frame of the window was made of fine black ebony, and as she sat looking out upon the snow, she pricked her finger, and three drops of blood fell upon it. Then she gazed thoughtfully upon the red drops that sprinkled the white snow, and said: 'Would that my little daughter may be as white as that snow, as red as that blood, and as black as this ebony window-frame!' And so the little girl really did grow up; her skin was as white as snow, her cheeks as rosy as the blood, and her hair as black as ebony; and she was called Snow-white.

But this queen died; and the king soon married another wife, who became queen, and was very beautiful, but so vain that she could not bear to think that any one could be handsomer than she was. She had a fairy looking-glass, to which she used to go, and then she would gaze upon herself in it, and say:

> 'Tell me, glass, tell me true!
> Of all the ladies in the land,
> Who is fairest? tell me, who?'

And the glass had always answered:

> 'Thou queen, art the fairest in all the land.'

But Snow-white grew more and more beautiful; and when she was seven years old she was as bright as the day, and fairer than the queen herself. Then the glass one day answered the queen, when she went to look in it as usual:

> 'Thou, queen, art fair, and beauteous to see,
> But Snow-white is lovelier far than thee!'

When she heard this she turned pale with rage and envy; and called to one of her servants and said: 'Take Snow-white away into the wide wood, that I may never see her any more.' Then the servant led her away; but his heart melted when Snow-white begged him to spare her life, and he said: 'I will not hurt thee, thou pretty child.' So he left her by herself; and though he thought it most likely that the wild beasts would tear her to pieces, he felt as if a great weight were taken off his heart when he had made up his mind not to kill her but to leave her to her fate, with the chance of someone finding her and saving her.

Then poor Snow-white wandered along through the wood in great fear; and the wild beasts roared about her, but none did her any harm. In the evening she came to a cottage among the hills; and went in to rest, for her little feet would carry her no further. Everything was spruce and neat in the cottage: on the table was spread a white cloth, and there were seven little plates, with seven little loaves, and seven little glasses with wine in them; and seven knives and forks laid in order; and by the wall stood seven little beds. As she was very hungry, she picked up a little piece off each loaf and drank a very little wine out of each glass; and after that she thought she would lie down and rest. So she tried all the little beds; but one was too long, and another was too short, till at last the seventh suited her: and there she laid herself down and went to sleep.

By and by in came the masters of the cottage. Now they were seven little dwarfs, that lived among the mountains, and dug and searched about for gold. They lighted up their seven lamps, and saw at once that all was not right.

The first said, 'Who has been sitting on my stool?'

The second, 'Who has been eating off my plate?'

The third, 'Who has been picking my bread?'

The fourth, 'Who has been meddling with my spoon?'

The fifth, 'Who has been handling my fork?'

The sixth, 'Who has been cutting with my knife?'

The seventh, 'Who has been drinking my wine?'

Then the first looked round and said, 'Who has been lying on my bed?' And the rest came running to him, and every one cried out that somebody had been upon his bed. But the seventh saw Snow-white, and called all his brethren to come and see her; and they cried out with wonder and astonishment and brought their lamps to look at her, and said: 'Good Heavens! what a lovely child she is!' And they were very glad to see her, and took care not to wake her; and the seventh dwarf slept an hour with each of the other dwarfs in turn, till the night was gone.

In the morning Snow-white told them all her story; and they pitied her, and said if she would keep all things in order, and cook and wash, and knit and spin for them, she might stay where she was, and they would take good care of her. Then they went out all day long to their work, seeking for gold and silver in the mountains; but Snow-white was left at home; and they warned her, and said: 'The queen will soon find out where you are, so take care and let no one in.'

But the queen, now that she thought Snow-white was dead, believed that she must be the handsomest lady in the land; and she went off to her glass and said:

> 'Tell me, glass, tell me true!
> Of all the ladies in the land,
> Who is fairest? tell me, who?'

And the glass answered:

> 'Thou, queen, art the fairest in all this land:
> But over the hills, in the greenwood shade,
> Where the seven dwarfs their dwelling have made,
> There Snow-white is hiding her head; and she
> Is lovelier far, O queen! than thee.'

Then the queen was very much frightened; for she knew that the glass always spoke the truth, and was sure that the servant had betrayed her. And she could not bear to think that any one lived who was more beautiful than she was; so she dressed herelf up as an old pedlar, and went her way over the hills, to the place where the dwarfs dwelt. Then she knocked at the door, and cried: 'Fine wares to sell!' Snow-white looked out at the window, and said: 'Good day, good woman! what have you to sell?' 'Good wares, fine wares,' said she; 'laces and bobbins of all colours.' 'I will let the old lady in; she seems to be a very good sort of body,' thought Snow-white; so she ran down and unbolted the door. 'Bless me!' said the old woman, 'how badly your stays are laced! Let me lace them up with one of my nice new laces.' Snow-white did not dream of any mischief; so she stood up before the old woman; but she set to work so nimbly, and pulled the lace so tight, that Snow-white's breath was stopped, and she fell down as if she were dead. 'There's an end to all thy beauty,' said the spiteful queen, and went away home.

In the evening the seven dwarfs came home; and I need not say how grieved they were to see their faithful Snow-white stretched out upon the ground, as if she were quite dead. However, they lifted her up, and when they found what ailed her, they cut the lace; and in a little time she began to breathe and very soon came to life again. Then they said: 'The old woman was the queen herself; take care another time, and let no one in when we are away.'

When the queen got home, she went straight to her glass, and spoke to it as before; but to her great grief it still said:

> 'Thou, queen, art the fairest in all this land:
> But over the hills, in the greenwood shade,
> Where the seven dwarfs their dwelling have made,
> There Snow-white is hiding her head; and she
> Is lovelier far, O queen! than thee.'

Then the blood ran cold in her heart with spite and malice, to see that Snow-white still lived; and she dressed herself again, but in quite another dress from the one she wore before, and took with her a poisoned comb. When she reached the dwarfs' cottage, she knocked at the door, and cried: 'Fine wares to sell!' But Snow-white said: 'I dare not let any one in.' Then the queen said: 'Only look at my beautiful combs!' and gave her the poisoned one. And it looked so pretty, that she took it up and put it into her hair to try it; but the moment it touched her head, the poison was so powerful that she fell down senseless. 'There you may lie,' said the queen, and went her way. But by good luck the dwarfs came in very early that evening; and when they saw Snow-white lying on the ground, they guessed what had happened, and soon found the poisoned comb. And when they took it away she got well, and told them all that had passed; and they warned her once more not to open the door to any one.

Meantime the queen went home to her glass, and shook with rage when she read the very same answer as before; and she said: 'Snow-white shall die, if it cost me my life.' So she went by herself into her chamber, and got ready a poisoned apple: the outside looked very rosy and tempting, but whoever tasted it was sure to die. Then she dressed herself up as a peasant's wife, and travelled over the hills to the dwarfs' cottage, and knocked at the door; but Snow-white put her head out of the window and said: 'I dare not let any one in, for the dwarfs have told me not. 'Do as you please,' said the old woman, 'but at any rate take this pretty apple; I will give it you.' 'No,' said Snow-white, 'I dare not take it.' 'You silly girl!' answered the other, 'what are you afraid of? Do you think it is poisoned? Come! do you eat one part, and I will eat the other.' Now the apple was so made up that one side was good, though the other was poisoned. Then Snow-white was much tempted to taste, for the apple looked so very nice; and when she saw the old woman eat, she could wait no longer. But she had scarcely put the piece into her mouth, when she fell down dead upon the ground. 'This time nothing will save thee,' said the queen; and she went home to her glass, and at last it said:

'Thou, queen, art the fairest of all the fair.'

And then her wicked heart was glad, and as happy as such a heart could be.

When evening came, and the dwarfs had got home, they

found Snow-white lying on the ground: no breath came from her lips, and they were afraid that she was quite dead. They lifted her up, and combed her hair, and washed her face with wine and water; but all was in vain, for the little girl seemed quite dead. So they laid her down upon a bier, and all seven watched and bewailed her three whole days; and then they thought they would bury her: but her cheeks were still rosy, and her face looked just as it did while she was alive; so they said: 'We will never bury her in the cold ground.' And they made a coffin of glass, so that they might still look at her, and wrote upon it in gold letters what her name was, and that she was a king's daughter. And the coffin was set among the hills, and one of the dwarfs always sat by it and watched. And the birds of the air came too, and bemoaned Snow-white; and first of all came an owl, and then a raven, and at last a dove, and sat by her side.

And thus Snow-white lay for a long, long time, and still only looked as though she were asleep; for she was even now as white as snow, and as red as blood, and as black as ebony. At last a prince came and called at the dwarfs' house; and he saw Snow-white, and read what was written in golden letters. Then he offered the dwarfs money, and prayed and besought them to let him take her away; but they said: 'We will not part with her for all the gold in the world.' At last however, they had pity on him, and gave him the coffin; but the moment he lifted it up to carry it home with him, the piece of apple fell from between her lips, and Snow-white awoke, and said: 'Where am I?' And the prince said: 'Thou art quite safe with me.'

Then he told her all that had happened, and said: 'I love you far better than all the world; so come with me to my father's palace, and you shall be my wife. And Snow-white consented, and went home with the prince;

and everything was got ready with great pomp and splendour for their wedding.

To the feast was asked, among the rest, Snow-white's old enemy the queen; and as she was dressing herself in fine rich clothes, she looked in the glass and said:

> 'Tell me, glass, tell me true!
> Of all the ladies in the land,
> Who is fairest? tell me, who?'

And the glass answered:

> 'Thou, lady, art loveliest here, I ween;
> But lovelier far is the new-made queen.'

When she heard this she started with rage; but her envy and curiosity were so great, that she could not help setting out to see the bride. And when she got there, and saw that it was no other than Snow-white, who, as she thought, had been dead a long while, she choked with rage, and fell down and died; but Snow-white and the prince lived and reigned happily over that land many, many years; and sometimes they went up into the mountains, and paid a visit to the little dwarfs, who had been so kind to Snow-white in her time of need.

# The Three Dwarfs in the Wood

THERE was once a man whose wife died and a woman whose husband died; the man had a daughter and the woman also had a daughter. These girls knew each other well; one day they went for a walk and then came into the woman's house. She said to the daughter of the man: 'Listen now: tell your father I would like to marry him, so that every morning you shall wash yourself in milk and have wine to drink; but my daughter shall wash in water and have water to drink.' The girl went home and told her father what the woman had said. The man said: 'What shall I do? Marriage is a joy and marriage is a torment too.' At last, since he could not make up his mind. he pulled one of his boots off and said: 'Take this boot. There is a hole in the sole. Take it into the loft and hang it on the big nail and pour water into it. If it holds water then I will marry again, but if it lets water I will not.' The girl did as she was bid, but the water swelled up the leather so that the hole was stopped and the water filled the boot up to the top. She told her father what had happened.

Then he went up himself, and when he saw that she was right he went and wooed the widow, and they were married.

The morning after, when the two girls got up, there was milk for the man's daughter to wash in and wine to drink; but for the woman's daughter there was water to wash in and water to drink. On the next morning there was water for the man's daughter as well as for the woman's daughter. And on the third morning there was water for washing and for drinking for the man's daughter, and milk to wash in and wine to drink for the woman's daughter, and so it went on, as on the third morning. The woman became spiteful towards her stepdaughter and could not think of enough ways to be unpleasant to her. She was jealous, too, because her stepdaughter was fair and lovely, but her own daughter ugly and hateful.

One day in winter, when it was freezing hard and the hills and valleys were covered in snow, the woman made a dress out of paper, and called her stepdaughter and said to her: 'Put this dress on, go into the forest, and get me a basket of strawberries; I have a fancy for some.'

'Oh dear,' said the girl, 'strawberries do not grow in winter, the earth is frozen and all covered with snow. Why must I go out in that paper dress? It's cold enough outside to freeze your breath. There is a wind blowing and the thorns will tear the dress off me.' 'Are you going to contradict me again?' asked her stepmother. 'Get along out with you, and don't let me see you again until you have filled this basket with strawberries.' Then she gave her a little bit of dry bread and said: 'That will last you all day,' thinking to herself: 'It will be freezing outside, and what with that and hunger I shall never set eyes on her again.'

So the girl did as she was bid; she put on the paper frock and went out with her little basket. Far and wide there was nothing to be seen but snow, and not so much as a blade of grass sticking through it.    When she got into the wood she saw a little house and three little old men looking out of it.    She passed the time of day with them, and knocked politely on the door.    They called to her to come in, and in she went and sat down on the bench before the stove, to warm herself and eat her breakfast.    The little old men said: 'Do give us some too.'    'Gladly,' she said, breaking her bread in two and giving them half.    'What are you doing here in the woods,' they asked, 'in that thin dress in the winter weather?'    'Ah,' she said, 'I am to get this basket full of strawberries, and I can't go home until I do.'    When she had eaten her bread they gave her a broom and said: 'Sweep the snow away from the back door with this.'    When she was outside the three little men said to each other: 'What shall we give her, for being so nice and kind and sharing her bread with us?'    The first one said: 'My present to her is that she shall grow more beautiful every day.'    The second one said: 'My present to her is that pieces of gold shall fall out of her mouth with every word she speaks.'    The third one said: 'My present to her is that a king shall come and make her his wife.'

But the young girl was doing as she was bid, and sweeping the snow away from behind the house; and what do you think she found?    Nothing more nor less than ripe strawberries, poking up dark red out of the snow.    In her joy she filled the basket, thanked the little men, shook them all by the hand, and ran home to bring her stepmother what she wanted.

As soon as she got inside the house and said 'Good evening' a gold piece fell out of her mouth.    Then she told what had happened to her in the woods, but at every word she said gold pieces fell out of her mouth, so that soon the room was paved with them. 'Now look how vain she is,' said her stepsister, 'throwing money away like that!' But secretly she was jealous and wanted to go to the woods too and pick strawberries. But her mother said: 'No, my dear daughter, it is too cold, you might freeze to death.' But as she would give her no peace she gave in in the end, sewed her a fine fur coat, which she made her put on, and gave her bread-and-butter and cake for her journey.

The girl went into the woods, straight up to the little house. The three little men were looking out as before, but she did not pass the time of day, and without looking at them or saying a word to them she stumped into the room, sat down in front of the stove, and began to eat her bread-and-butter and cake. 'Give us some too,' cried the little men, but she answered: 'There's not even enough for me; how can I give some to any one else?' When she had finished eating they said: 'Here is a broom, now sweep the snow away from our back door.' 'Sweep for yourselves,' she said, 'I am not your servant.' When she saw that they would not give her anything, she went out of the door. Then the little men said to each other: 'What shall we give her for being so hasty and unkind of heart, too mean to give any one anything?' The first said: 'My present to her is that she shall grow uglier every day.' The second one said: 'My present to her is, that with every word she speaks a toad shall fall out of her mouth.' The third one said: 'My present to her is, that she shall die an unhappy death.' Outside the girl was looking for strawberries, but when she found none she went angrily home. When she opened her mouth to tell her mother what had happened to her in the woods a toad fell out of her mouth at every word she spoke, so that every one was sickened at the sight of them.

Now the stepmother became angrier than ever, and all she thought of was how to make life miserable for her husband's daughter, whose beauty grew greater every day. At last she took a pot, put it on the fire, and boiled some yarn in it. When it was boiled she hung it on her stepdaughter's shoulder, gave her an axe, and told her to go to the frozen river, cut a hole in the ice, and wash the yarn. She did as she was bid, went and chopped a hole in the ice, and as she was chopping away a splendid carriage came by, with the king sitting in it. The carriage stopped, and the king asked: 'Who are you, my child, and what are you doing here?' 'I am a poor girl washing yarn.' The king pitied her, and seeing that she was so beautiful he said: 'Would you like to ride along with me?' 'Oh yes, with all my heart,' she answered, for she was glad to get out of sight of her mother and sister.

So she got into the carriage and off she set with the king, and when they reached his castle their wedding was held with great splendour, just as the three little men had wished. A year later the young queen had a little son, and when her stepmother heard of this good fortune she came to the castle with her own daughter as if she was on a visit. But as soon as the king had gone out and there was no one about, the wicked woman seized the queen by her hair and her daughter seized her by the feet, and they lifted her out of bed and threw her out of the window into a stream that ran underneath it. Then she put her ugly daughter into the bed, and the old woman pulled the sheets over her head. When the king came back and wanted to talk to his wife the old woman said: 'Be quiet, you cannot speak to her now, she is in a heavy sweat; you must let her rest quietly to-day.' The king saw nothing amiss and did not come back until the next morning. When he spoke to his wife

and she answered him, at every word a toad fell out of her
mouth, whereas before gold pieces had fallen out. He
asked what this meant, but the old woman said it was
because of the heavy sweat she had had, and it would soon
pass.

Now that night the kitchen-boy saw a duck come swimming up the drain, and it said:

> 'How now, lord king,
> Art asleep or waking?'

When he gave no answer it asked:

> 'What of my guests?'

The kitchen-boy answered:

> 'Asleep in their nests.'

The duck asked again:

> 'And what of my little son?'

He answered:

> 'Asleep, like every one.'

Then the duck took on the form of the queen, and gave the
baby a drink, shook up his little bed, tucked him in, and
swam away back down the drain in the form of a duck.

So she came again a second night, but on the third night
she said to the kitchen-boy: 'Go and tell the king to take
his sword and brandish it over me three times on the
threshold.' Then the boy ran and told the king, who came
with his sword and brandished it three times over her; and
the third time there stood his queen in front of him, alive
and well as she had been before.

Now the king was overjoyed, but he kept the queen
hidden in a room until the Sunday on which the baby was

to be christened.   After the christening he said: 'What does a person deserve who has hauled someone out of bed and thrown them into the water?'   'Nothing better,' answered the old woman, 'than to be shut up in a tub with spikes inside it and rolled downhill into the water.'

Then the king said: 'You have pronounced your own doom.'   He had such a tub brought, and the mother and daughter put inside; then it was nailed up and the tub rolled downhill into the river.

# The Four Craftsmen

'DEAR children,' said a poor man to his four sons, 'I have nothing to give you; you must go out into the wide world and try your luck. Begin by learning some craft or another, and see how you can get on.' So the four brothers took their walking-sticks in their hands, and their little bundles on their shoulders, and after bidding their father good-bye, went all out at the gate together. When they had got on some way they came to four cross-ways, each leading to a different country. Then the eldest said: 'Here we must part; but this day four years we will come back to this spot, and in the meantime each must try what he can do for himself.'

So each brother went his way; and as the eldest was hastening on a man met him, and asked him where he was going, and what he wanted. 'I am going to try my luck in the world, and should like to begin by learning some art or trade,' answered he. 'Then,' said the man, 'go with me, and I will teach you how to become the cunningest thief that ever was.' 'No,' said the other, 'that is not an honest calling, and what can one look to earn by it in the end but the gallows?' 'Oh!' said the man, 'you need not fear the gallows, for I will only teach you to steal what will be fair game: I meddle with nothing but what no one else can get or care anything about, and where no one can find you out.' So the young man agreed to follow his trade, and he soon showed himself so clever, that nothing could escape him that he had once set his mind upon.

The second brother also met a man, who, when he found out what he was setting out upon, asked him what craft he meant to follow. 'I do not know yet,' said he. 'Then come with me, and be a star-gazer. It is a noble art, for nothing can be hidden from you, when once you understand the stars.' The plan pleased him much, and he soon became a skilful star-gazer, that when he had served out his time, and wanted to leave his master, he gave him a glass, and said: 'With this you can see all that is passing in the sky and on earth, and nothing can be hidden from you.'

The third brother met a huntsman, who took him with

him, and taught him so well all that belonged to hunting, that he became very clever in the craft of the woods; and when he left his master he gave him a bow, and said: 'Whatever you shoot at with this bow you will be sure to hit.'

The youngest brother likewise met a man who asked him what he wished to do. 'Would not you like,' said he, 'to be a tailor?' 'Oh, no!' said the young man; 'sitting cross-legged from morning to night, working backwards and forwards with a needle and goose, will never suit me.' 'Oh!' answered the man, 'that is not my sort of tailoring; come with me, and you will learn quite another kind of craft from that.' Not knowing what better to do, he came into the plan, and learnt tailoring from the beginning; and when he left his master he gave him a needle, and said: 'You can sew anything with this, be it as soft as an egg or as hard as steel; and the joint will be so fine that no seam will be seen.'

After the space of four years, at the time agreed upon, the four brothers met at the four cross-roads; and having welcomed each other, set off towards their father's home, where they told him all that had happened to them, and how each had learned some craft.

Then, one day, as they were sitting before the house under a very high tree, the father said: 'I should like to try what each of you can do in this way.' So he looked up, and said to the second son: 'At the top of this tree there is a chaffinch's nest; tell me how many eggs there are in it.' The star-gazer took his glass, looked up, and said, 'Five.' 'Now,' said the father to the eldest son, 'take away the eggs without letting the bird that is sitting upon them and hatching them know anything of what you are doing.' So the cunning thief climbed up the tree, and brought away to his father the five eggs from under the bird; and it never saw or felt what he was doing, but kept sitting on at its ease. Then the father took the eggs, and put one on each corner of the table, and the fifth in the middle; and said to the huntsman: 'Cut all the eggs in two pieces at one shot.' The huntsman took up his bow, and at one shot struck all the five eggs as his father wished. 'Now comes your turn,' said he to the young tailor; 'sew the eggs and the young birds in them together again, so neatly that the shot shall have done them no harm.' Then the tailor took his needle, and sewed the eggs as he was told; and when he had done, the thief was sent to take them back to the nest, and put them under the bird without its knowing it. Then she went on sitting, and hatched them: and in a few days they crawled out, and had only a little red streak across their necks, where the tailor had sewn them together.

'Well done, sons!' said the old man: 'you have made good use of your time, and learnt something worth the knowing; but I am sure I do not know which ought to have the prize. Oh! that a time might soon come for you to turn your skill to some account!'

Not long after this there was a great bustle in the country; for the king's daughter had been caried off by a mighty dragon, and the king mourned over his loss day and night, and made it known that whoever brought her back to him should have her for a wife. Then the four brothers said to each other: 'Here is a chance for us; let us try what we can do.' And they agreed to see whether they could not set the princess free. 'I will soon find out where she is, however,' said the star-gazer, as he looked through his glass; and he soon cried out: 'I see her afar off, sitting upon a rock in the sea; and I can spy the dragon close by, guarding her.' Then he went to the king, and asked for a ship for himself and his brothers; and they sailed together over the sea, till they came to the right place. There they found the princess sitting, as the star-gazer had said, on the rock; and the dragon was lying asleep, with his head upon her lap. 'I dare not shoot him,' said the huntsman, 'for I should kill the beautiful maiden also.' 'Then I will try my skill,' said the thief; and went and stole her away from under the dragon, so quietly and gently that the beast did not know it, but went on snoring.

Then away they hastened with her full of joy in their boat towards the ship; but soon came the dragon roaring behind them through the air; for he awoke and missed the princess. But when he got over the boat, and wanted to pounce upon them and carry off the princess, the huntsman took up his bow and shot him straight through the heart, so that he fell down dead. They were still not safe; for he was such a great beast that in his fall he overset the boat, and they had to swim in the open sea upon a few planks. So the tailor took his needle, and with a few large stitches put some of the planks together; and he sat down upon these, and sailed about and gathered up all the pieces of the boat; and then tacked them together so quickly that the boat was soon ready, and then they reached the ship and got home safe.

When they had brought home the princess to her father, there was great rejoicing; and he said to the four brothers: 'One of you shall marry her, but you must settle among yourselves which it is to be.' Then there arose a quarrel between them; and the star-gazer said: 'If I had not found the princess out, all your skill would have been of no use; therefore she ought to be mine.' 'Your seeing her would have been of no use,' said the thief, 'if I had not taken her away from the dragon; therefore she ought to be mine.' 'No, she is mine,' said the huntsman; 'for if I had not killed the dragon, he would, after all, have torn you and the princess into pieces.' 'And if I had not sewn the boat together again,' said the tailor, 'you would all have been drowned; therefore she is mine.' Then the king put in a word, and said: 'Each of you is right; and as all cannot have the princess, the best way is for none of you to have her; for the truth is, there is somebody she likes a great deal better. But to make up for your loss, I will give each of you, as a reward for his skill, half a kingdom.' So the brothers agreed that this plan would be much better than either quarrelling or marrying a lady who had no mind to have them. And the king then gave to each half a kingdom, as he had said, and they lived very happily the rest of their days, and took good care of their father; and somebody took better care of the princess, than to let either the dragon or one of the craftsmen have her again.

# Snow-White & Rose-Red

A POOR woman once lived in a lonely little cottage with a garden in front of it; in the garden were two rose-bushes, one with white and one with red flowers. She had two children that were like the two rose-bushes; one was called Snow-white and the other Rose-red. Now they were as good and well-behaved, they worked as hard and as cheerfully as any two children that ever were seen: but Snow-white was quieter and more gentle than Rose-red, who would rather be running about the woods and fields, picking flowers and catching butterflies. But Snow-white would sit at home with her mother and help her in the house or read to her if she had nothing else to do.

The two children were so fond of each other that they always went about hand-in-hand: and as often as Snow-white said: 'We will never part,' Rose-red would answer: 'Not as long as we live,' and their mother would add: 'You must

159

share and share alike.' They often used to go rambling off together in the forest, picking wild berries; but none of the beasts harmed them; on the contrary, they came confidently right up to them, so that the little hares would eat cabbage leaves out of their hands and the roebuck graze beside them, while the stag galloped gaily past and the little birds sitting on the boughs sang all the songs they knew. No harm came to them; if they were out late in the forest and night overtook them, they would lie down side by side on the moss and sleep till morning; and their mother knew this was so and did not worry about them. Once, when they had been spending the night in the woods and awoke with the dawn they saw a most beautiful child dressed in a shining white robe sitting beside the place where they lay. The child stood up and looked at them in a friendly way, but said nothing and went into the wood. When they looked round they saw that they had been sleeping on the edge of a precipice, down which they would certainly have fallen if they had gone a few steps further in the dark. Their mother told them it must have been the angel that looks after good children.

Snow-white and Rose-red kept their mother's cottage so clean it was a pleasure to look inside it. In the summer Rose-red looked after the house, and every morning before her mother woke she put a bunch of flowers by her bedside, containing a rose from each of the bushes. In winter Snow-white lit the fire and hung the kettle on the pot-hook, shining like gold, although it was only brass. In the evening, when the snow was falling, her mother would say: 'Snow-white, go and shoot the bolts,' and then they would sit down in front of the fire and their mother would put on her glasses and read to them out of a big book, and the two girls would listen as they sat spinning; a lamb lay beside

them on the floor, and behind them on his perch sat a white
dove with his head tucked under his wing.

One evening, as they were sitting snugly round the fire,
there was a knock at the door, as if someone wanted to come
in.   Their mother said: 'Be quick, Rose-red, and open the
door, it must be someone who wants to rest here for the
night.'   Rose-red got up and drew the bolts, thinking it
must be some poor man; but it was no such thing, but a
bear, who stuck his great black head inside the door.

Rose-red screamed and jumped backwards; the lamb
bleated, the dove fluttered away, and Snow-white hid behind
her mother's bed.   But the bear opened his mouth and said:
'Don't be afraid; I won't hurt you, I 'm half frozen, and I
only want to get warm at your fire for a while.'

'Poor bear,' said their mother, 'lie down by the fire, and
take care you don't burn your coat.'   Then she called:
'Come out, Snow-white and Rose-red.   The bear won't do
you any harm; he means well.'   Then they both came back,
and gradually the lamb and the dove too came back to their
places without fear of the bear.   The bear said: 'Now
children, just knock some of the snow off my coat,' and
they fetched a broom and brushed the snow out of his fur,
while he lay in front of the fire grunting with pleasure and
well-being.   It was not long before they were so confident
that they did what they liked with their uninvited guest.
They pulled his hair, put their feet on his back and wiped
them, or took a hazel-rod and poked him till he growled,
which made them laugh.   The bear put up with it all,
only when it got too much for him he cried out: 'Leave
me alone, children!

> 'Snow-white, Rose-red,
>   Don't strike your lover dead.'

When it was time to go to bed, and the others had retired,

the mother said to the bear: 'You are welcome to stay here by the fire; you will be safe from the cold and rough weather there.' As soon as it was morning the two children let him out, and he trotted off over the snow to the forest. From that time forward the bear began to come every evening at the same time, lay down in front of the fire, and allowed the children to play with him as much as they liked; and they grew so used to him that they never bolted the door until their black friend had arrived.

Now when spring had come and all the leaves were green, the bear said to Snow-white one fine morning: 'Now I must go away and I shall not be coming again all summer.' 'Where are you going, dear bear?' she asked. 'I must go to the forest and guard my treasure against the wicked dwarfs: in winter, when the ground is hard with frost, they have to stay underground and can't dig their way out; but now that the sun has warmed and thawed the earth they will be able to break out and come up picking and stealing; if they once get their hands on anything and get it as far as their caves it will be a long time before it sees the light of day again.' Snow-white was quite sad at parting, and when she opened the door for him and he bundled out he caught a bit of his fur on the hasp; it tore off, and it seemed to her as if she saw the glint of gold underneath it; but she could not be certain. The bear ran away in haste, and was soon out of sight behind the trees.

After a little while the mother sent her children into the forest to gather firewood. They found a great tree lying on the ground, and by its stump something was jumping up and down, but they could not make out what it was. But when they drew nearer they saw it was a dwarf with a shrivelled old face and a beard a yard long, as white as snow. The end of his beard was stuck fast in a cleft in the fallen tree, and the little man was jumping about like a dog on a lead and quite helpless. He stared at the girls with his red fiery eyes and shouted at them: 'What are you standing there for? Can't you come here and help me?' 'What have you been doing, little man?' asked Rose-red. 'You silly inquisitive goose,' answered the dwarf, 'I was going to split the tree up for firewood for my kitchen; just a few splinters. These great chunks of wood are apt to burn the little snacks the likes of us eat; we don't need the great meals you coarse, greedy people swallow. I had managed to drive the wedge in all right, and all was going well, when the wet slimy wood slipped, curse it, and I wasn't prepared for it. I had no time to pull back my beautiful white beard before the wood closed on it. Now it's stuck and I can't move. And all you stupid, milk-white smooth-faces can do is laugh. Pooh, you nasty things!'

The children tried and tried, but the beard was stuck fast and they could not pull it out. 'I'll run and fetch some people,' said Rose-red. 'Stupid oafs!' snarled the dwarf, 'who wants more people? You are two too many already. Can't you think of anything better than that?' 'Now don't be impatient,' said she, 'I'll think of something.' She took her scissors out of her pocket and cut off the end of his beard. As soon as the dwarf was loose he snatched up a sack full of gold from between the roots of the tree and as he picked it up he grumbled to himself: 'What rude people! Cut off a bit of my beard! The devil pay them for it!' He swung the sack over his shoulder and went off without another glance at the children.

Some time after that Snow-white and Rose-red went out to catch a few fish. When they got to the stream, they saw something like a big grasshopper hopping towards the bank as if it were going to jump into the water. They ran up to it and found the dwarf. 'What are you doing?' asked Rose-red. 'Surely you're not going to jump into the water?' 'I'm not such a fool,' shouted the dwarf. 'Can't you see the cursed fish is trying to pull me in?' The little man had been sitting there with rod and line, and an unlucky gust of wind had tangled his beard up in the line: straight away he had a bite, and was not strong enough to pull the big fish out. The fish got the better of things and was dragging the dwarf towards him. Despite his hanging on to every tuft of grass and bent, he had to yield to the fish and was in imminent danger of being dragged into the water. The girls arrived in the nick of time to hold him steady, and they tried to disentangle his beard from the line, but without success; beard and line were too firmly knotted together. There was nothing for it but to bring out the little scissors again and cut his beard loose, so that a small part of it was lost. When the dwarf saw that, he shouted: 'Is that the way to treat people's faces, you toadstools? You are not content with docking the end off my beard but you must cut the better part of it off as well. Now I shan't be able to show my face before my own people. I wish you would run away barefoot!' Then he picked up a sack of pearls that was lying in the rushes, and without another word dragged it away and disappeared round a stone.

It so happened that soon after that their mother sent the sisters to the town to buy needles, thread, laces, and ribbons. The road led over the moor, which was strewn here and there with great fragments of stone. They saw a great bird wheeling about in the air; it sailed slowly over their heads, diving lower and lower, and finally pitched beside a rock quite near them. Immediately they heard a piercing, pitiful cry. They ran to the spot and were astonished to see that the eagle had seized their old friend the dwarf and was about to carry him off. The children had pity on the little man and caught hold of him and tugged away until the eagle let go his prize. When the dwarf had got over the first shock, he cried in a rasping voice: 'Could you not have handled me more carefully? You have grabbed at my thin jacket until it is all tattered and torn, you clumsy, stupid boobies!' Then he picked up a sack full of gems and slipped away between the rocks to his cave.

The girls had by now got used to his ingratitude; they went on their way and got their business done in the town. When they were crossing the moor on their way back, they surprised the dwarf, who had spread out his gems on a level bit of ground and was not expecting any one to come along so late. The evening sun touched the glittering jewels so that they flashed and glowed so splendidly in all their colours that the children stood still to watch them. 'Why are you standing there gaping like asses?' cried the dwarf, and his ashen-grey face went as red as cinnabar with rage. He would have gone on scolding them, but a low growling was heard and a black bear came trotting out of the woods. The dwarf jumped up in terror, but he could not get to his hiding place, for the bear was close upon him. In the anguish of his fear he cried out: 'Dear bear, forgive me, I will give you all my treasures; see the pretty gems lying here. Spare my life; what good would a little wizened fellow like me be to eat? You would not taste me between your teeth. Here, take these two naughty girls, they'll make you a tasty morsel, fat as young quails; you're welcome to eat them.' The bear took no notice of his words but gave the vicious creature one clout with his paw that stretched him lifeless.

The children had run away, but the bear called after them: 'Snow-white, Rose-red, don't be afraid, wait for me.' Then they recognized his voice and stopped, and when the bear came up with them his skin fell off him, and he stood before them a handsome man, dressed all in cloth-of-gold. 'I am a king's son,' said he. 'But that nasty dwarf stole my treasure from me and put a spell on me to make me run about the woods in the shape of a bear until his death should set me free. Now he has reaped his just deserts.'

Snow-white married him and Rose-red married his brother, and they shared between them the great treasure that the dwarf had heaped up in his cave. Their old mother lived with them quietly and happily for many years after that. But she took both her rose-trees with her and they were planted in front of her window, and every year they bore roses, the one white and the other red.